THE OLDEST TRICK IN THE BOOK

Book Three of the "Never Too Old" Western Series

J.V. JAMES

Classic West Tales

DEDICATION

for all horses
plain or grand, wild or tame, fast or slow

CONTENTS

CHAPTER 1
AT LEAST TRAIN ROBBERS MAKE TRAVEL FUN
SEPTEMBER, 1878. CHEYENNE, WYOMING TERRITORY

T rains is trains, and comforts is comforts — and if you hope for the second, you best keep away from the first.

Only fun part of the journey was when a few young fools tried to rob us. Them boys thought they was God's gift to train robberies, and had such a flair for it us passengers would enjoy being robbed. It sure takes all types, don't it?

Anyway, they sure weren't the James-Younger Gang, and it didn't go quite how they planned.

But we'll get to all that in a moment.

The first leg of our journey had been just about bearable. From Santa Monica to San Francisco, we played a sort of a game, looking out at the scenery for things that had changed this past year — or trying to be first to spy the ocean when it came into view, as it quite often did.

Mary and Georgina won the game mostly — me, I was

just happy to be there beside 'em, the best little daughter and wife a man could be blessed with.

We spent a day and a night in San Francisco before boarding the train that would take us all the way to Cheyenne. That long day and night confirmed that famous wild city is not so much a place people *live,* but more like a sort of *purgatory for the damned.*

Stark raving loco, each man who lives in that place, and we three were all glad to escape it.

Sixty dollars for uncomfortable beds, and fifty for a meal that may not have been actual food. A whole city gone crazy on gold dust, and forgetting to look out for each other as they all try to claw out a living.

By the time I loaded our horses onto the train the next morning, I'd decided to never set foot in the dang place again.

When our train pulled away, we were excited to be headed to Cheyenne. At the least, we'd catch up with old friends — and perhaps we'd even track down the man who had killed Mary's parents two years ago.

Excited as we were, we had forgotten how unpleasant train travel could be.

Despite spending extra for beds in a sleeper car, we found ourselves exhausted by the second day's travel.

The endless rattling, bumping and jolting, the stench of the coal-smoke, and the contagious anxiety of our fellow passengers did not *really* bother me much — but the boredom, the endless damn boredom of mile upon mile of nothing-to-do, that's what I could not stand.

There's only two places worth sitting, I reckon — the

first is always worth a *short* sit, it's called a dinner table. And the other's worth sitting much longer — that's the back of a horse. But these dang train seats weren't nothing more than long days of torture.

But then, finally — finally! — SOMETHING was going to happen.

A sudden sense of life having stopped, or faltered at least, was how it began.

The endless push and forward grind of the train was no longer there — it had not slowed the way it does when deliberately stopping, but had simply lost all propulsion.

A little like floating through air, when you're throwed by a horse, unexpected.

And this too, might be painful when we came to the end of it.

Well, pain's best avoided where possible — and we was prepared for such things as might happen during our journey. At least, I hoped we was prepared. I was anyway.

We were in the dining car partaking of breakfast. I was facing our direction of travel with Georgina beside me, and Mary sitting opposite to us, facing the back of the carriage. There's reasons for that.

We'd made a start on the food. Eggs, bacon, grits and biscuits. Not bad — not good neither.

There was a dozen other people in the dining car, it being still early, and train travelers leaning to lazy, I guess. About a third-full was all, at this hour. City folk mostly, they were, heading back East with their tails 'tween their legs, or going somewhere on business. Not one of 'em likely to be useful, if a frolic got started.

"Feel that?" I said quietly.

Mary crinkled her nose and cocked her head sideways before answering. "Feel what, Father?"

"Trouble," I said, and tapped her twice on her wrist, a signal I'd taught her which meant *Draw your pistol but keep the thing hidden.*

Mary's eyes widened, but she took out her little Sharps derringer, rested that hand on the table in front of her, and dropped a napkin over the top of it — all without anyone seeing.

Anyone but me and my wife, a'course.

As for my beautiful wife, I would not let Georgina touch a gun within range of another human being, lest we *all* end up shot accidental. She looked at me quizzical now, but I only said, "If anything happens, get your head down and leave it to us."

Mary blinked hard and said, "Father, I don't know if I..."

And as her voice trailed off I said, "Mary, remember to breathe, nice and calm. And only go on my signal, or if we're in danger. I got faith in you, girl."

Then the door at the front of the carriage flew open, and a skinny masked feller strode in waving a six-gun.

"Good morning, folks," shouted the fool through his flashy bright red bandana. "And con-gratter-layshuns. You's the first folks ever to get robbed by the famous Friend Gang."

Dang fool kid, I thought to myself. *Fifteen at the eldest, and unlikely to make sixteen at this rate.*

One older lady squealed a little, while a youngish pencil-necked suit-wearin' feller threw his hands in the air though he hadn't been told to. Suited me fine, as these two attracted Red Bandana's attention.

He had paused a few moments for effect, waved the gun round some more, then went on. "Now if it ain't no trouble, please take out your money and jewels and such like, and my friend back there will collect it all up in his hat."

For a first thing, that just ain't how it's done. He shoulda had us all put our hands up where he could see 'em — instead of letting us keep our hands on our guns.

Small point that, but proper robbers think it important.

And for a second thing, he might shoulda looked through the carriage beforehand in order to see who was in it.

Dang fool mighta seen Lyle Frakes, and altered his plan.

Well, I just gently placed my moccasined foot on top of Mary's toes and sat real quiet, with my fingers curled around Wilma, under the table, pointed right at that fool's red bandana. *Wilma's my Remington Rider — five shots of death for anyone fool enough to annoy her.*

Mary tapped my moccasin once with her other foot, letting me know there was only one feller at her end to deal with.

Young Red Bandana moved toward us a little, and I was then able to see past him through the open doorway he'd entered from.

Instead of seeing the rest of our train, I seen there was nothin' else out there but *air* — he had pulled out the pin that secured the dining car to the carriage in front of us. The engine had chugged away round a bend, leaving nothing but a slowly rising black cloud for evidence.

We were still coasting along, but down to a slow horse's trotting speed, more-or-less.

"In the hat please, folks," called the feller behind me, as the one in front finally got around to looking at me proper.

He made a big show of waving the gun around — like a damn fool who'd never robbed nothin' before in his life and was only play-acting — and said, "You. Old man. Why ain't you gettin' your cash out and ready? By the time my friends rob the mail car, we gots to get going, we ain't got all day."

I tapped Mary's foot and she tapped right back, and I said, "Boy, I don't know who you are, but I do know you're a dang fool. You best drop that gun and walk backways outta here now, or you'll die right there where you're standing."

Fool kid roared with laughter, waved his Colt around again, and said, "We're the Friend Gang, old man, and we's gonna be famouser'n the—"

That's when Mary kicked my foot hard, and the both of us fired and fired again, as folks started screaming and yelling and hitting the floor.

My first bullet hit young Red Bandana's gun hand, and my second hit his leg as he tried to jump backways and sideways. As for his six-gun, it went flying right out of a window and the poor fool kid squealed like a stuck hog.

Mary's feller had cried out when she fired and he too fumbled his gun. Then he'd threw the hatful of valuables at her, and ran back out the door, calling *"RUN,"* to all his compadres. "You shot me, mister, you shot me," cried Red Bandana, as I jumped up outta my seat and walked to him, with Wilma pointed right at his face.

"On your feet, you damn fool," I said.

"I can't believe you shot me, what's wrong with you, old man? Dammit, first robbery ever, and I'm gonna die."

"Stay in your seat, Mary, but shoot anyone who comes through that door," I called behind me, and I looked out the window.

"RUN FOR IT, BOYS, they all got guns," Mary's feller was yelling as he scrambled and tumbled end-for-end down the rocky slope, raising dust.

Well, he didn't need to tell *them*.

The others had all hightailed it soon as they heard our shots, and were running toward a half-growed little feller — *no older than Mary I reckon* — who was holding their horses in readiness for a quick getaway.

"It's your lucky day," I told Red Bandana, as I grabbed his collar and dragged the young fool to his feet.

He was staring wide-eyed at his left hand, which was missing the end of its thumb, and he hadn't even noticed the outside of his thigh had been grazed. Not *much* blood there, but *some,* seeping out through his britches — so, lucky for him, just a flesh wound.

I dragged the kid by his ear to the doorway, pushed him out onto the tracks in a limb-tangled heap, and said, "You best get to your horse, son, here comes the engine, and the guard ain't likely to treat you so nicely as I have."

He looked behind him then, seen the rest a'the train as it came backing round the bend into sight, then looked up at me and said, in a real small voice, "Sorry, mister. It weren't my idea."

And I said, "Learn the lesson, son, and don't ever do it again — you *or* your friends. And if ever I hear of a wrongdoer missin' a thumb tip, I'll hunt you down and put the next one right through your brainpan. Now git."

And young Red Bandana jumped to his feet, and got gittin' while the gittin' was good.

CHAPTER 3
HAND IN YOUR GUNS

Under a glaring mid-morning sun, three days after leaving San Francisco, our train finally chugged into Cheyenne. The squeal of brakes and the blowing off of steam was a welcome noise by this time — I felt comforted that it was over, would be my main meaning — but such sounds as it made were almost drowned out by the grumbling of dissatisfied passengers.

People sure have gotten soft, these modern times, myself included.

All us complainers should try driving a wagon that same twelve-hundred miles, and see how our rumps feel after six weeks of *that* sort of jarring.

Train ain't my favorite thing, but I sure do appreciate its speed.

While I unloaded our horses, Georgina and Mary wandered along to my usual hotel and booked us a room.

Having done this same trip in reverse just a year ago,

our animals was all seasoned travelers, and had pulled up just fine. Didn't hurt that I'd spent parts of the trip in the stock car with them, and been sure to feed and water 'em proper during the journey.

"See that, Horse?" I said, pointing out the bright red letters on a over-large sign. *"Hand in Your Guns.* Not, *Hope You Had a Pleasant Journey,* or *Welcome to Cheyenne.* Ain't even at our hotel room yet, and bein' bossed about by the Law."

Horse didn't seem to care, and neither did Dewdrop or Gray, so I tied them together and led them along the street til we came to the good Livery.

"Mister Frakes," called young Roy Grimm from inside, and he limped out into the sunlight to help with the horses. "It's sure good to see you. You come to town for the big horse race?"

"Just got some business in town, Roy," I answered, shaking his hand. "Never knew there was a race on. Don't reckon this ol' bag'a'bones here could beat a turtle round a track anyway. Leastways not if it was in training."

Roy ran his hands over Dewdrop, checking her out as he spoke, way a good horseman does, even though I'd not asked him to. "You're lucky you got here today, Mister Frakes — another day or two there won't be an empty stable in town. It's like a traveling circus now, pretty much, and fair prizemoney too for the cup race. Yesterday they raced in Sidney, so soon as the train comes today there'll be thoroughbreds everywhere."

We gabbed about this and that as we cared for the

horses, and it turned out young Roy had got himself hitched a few months back.

"About time," I told him. "You must be near thirty by now."

"Yessir," he said, "I'm thirty-three. You just wait til you meet her, Mister Frakes, she's the prettiest and cleverest little filly ever walked on two legs, and I got you to thank for it too."

I looked over at him with my best alarmed look and said, "Steady on, Roy, don't blame me for your troubles. One thing to rush into marriage, another thing to blame some *other* innocent victim of that great institution."

"Aw, Mister Frakes," he laughed, "you always was the wisest feller I knew. But last year, when you started callin' me by my right name instead a'calling me Limpy way everyone else does, I decided you was right about all that. I took to standin' up for myself. Got in a few scuffles and scrapes, but now just about everyone calls me by my right name. And I got a wife from it too."

I smiled at him and said, "So you knew her already, I guess, and she grew some respect for you, on account of you standing up for yourself?"

"Well, not that exactly," he replied. "I had it out with my brothers, you see? Told 'em they best call me Roy from then on, or I'd take it out on their hides."

"Mean fellers, them brothers a'yours, from what I remember."

"Most specially mean when they're drunk, Mister Frakes — which they were. Upshot was, they kept callin' me Limpy, and we had it out once and for all."

"And?"

"When I woke up in the Hospital, there lookin' into my eyes was the prettiest and cleverest and caring-est filly I ever laid eyes on. We was married a month later, and them dang brothers a'mine are the only ones who still call me Limpy."

CHAPTER 4

THE STORY OF RED'S FINAL
MOMENTS

"Handsome Roy!" cried Mary as she rushed into the Livery, dragging Georgina along by the hand. "Look, Mother, this is the handsome liveryman I told you about."

I saved the suddenly crimson-faced Roy from his embarrassment by saying, "Georgina, this is Roy Grimm, the best man with a horse this side a'Montana. Roy, this is my wife, Georgina."

"Pleased to meet you, Roy," she said, coming over and shaking his hand. "Are you *always* called Handsome Roy?"

"Only by Miss Mary," he said, fiddling some with his collar. "And sometimes by my wife, when she's in a real good mood."

Mary's mouth opened wide in surprise, then she smiled like she'd struck gold. "You're *married*, Handsome Roy? Well, of course I knew you would be, a fellow like you. I'd best strike your name from my list then. I suspect I might marry Squirrel now anyway, oh, you should see him, he's *ever* so—"

"You stop that now, Mary," I told her. "You got ten, fifteen years 'fore you start worryin' on such things."

"I'll be an old maid in ten years," she said, throwing her arms about Dewdrop's neck and breathing in the scent of the horse. Then she turned to Roy and added, "I'm already ten, Handsome Roy. Almost a grown-up lady."

"You sure are, Miss Mary," he said.

Deciding it was time to save Roy from Mary, I said, "You know whether Deputy Slaughter's working today?"

"Saw him heading home when I opened this morning, Mister Frakes. Fact is, Emmett told me you might be arriving sometime this week, and to save you some stables if I could. He told me if you turn up today I should send you all out to see him, if you feel up to it."

I looked at Georgina and she nodded agreement, and Mary was just about jumping with excitement already.

We saddled the horses for the short trip, and said our goodbyes to Roy.

A few minutes later we rode into Emmett Slaughter's yard. He had painted the house since I'd seen it, and his wife had a good garden growing in well-tended rows. House was a shining white now with red trim, the post and rail front fence was all painted white too, and the gate was brand new — best part was, you didn't have to step down off your horse to open that wide swinging gate. There was even a catch to keep it open while you went through, before it closed itself on a spring.

Mighty fancy improvements, some folks can make in a year.

Oh, and his children had growed some as well.

Young Emmett was snoozing on his porch rocker when we arrived — but typical of a good Deputy, he was a light sleeper.

Looked up at us and a smile spread over his face, then he called out, "Company, Jeanie. It's the Frakes family."

"Emmett," I said, greeting him with a nod. "You know Mary already, a'course, and the fine lady riding the gray is Georgina."

"Morning, Mary," he said. "And it's very nice to meet you, Mrs Frakes. This is my wife, Jeanie, and those wild things climbing the tree are our children, Betty and Sam. Well, step on down, friends, don't just sit there on your horses!"

Seemed like we was expected — Jeanie had made a big lunch, and it was a good one. You'd go a long way to find a tastier meal of black-tailed deer, beans, potatoes and carrots.

She allowed her own children to eat on the steps, so the rest of us could talk freely of things they was too young to hear.

And a good thing she did — while we gobbled up that fine meal, Emmett filled us in on all that he knew about the murder of Mary's parents.

Turned out that the dying man, Red Abbott, was a member of a family who owned one of the Liveries in town. Far as Emmett knew, Red had never been in no trouble before, so it had been a surprise when the Sheriff called in every Deputy he had — and a posse as well — and told them to shoot Red on sight.

"Your boss, the County Sheriff, Cal Pettygore?"

"That's him, Lyle," said Emmett.

"Just makin' sure that ain't changed since last I was here."

Emmett nodded a grim one and went on. "Sheriff Pettygore told us all that Red fit the description of a man who robbed a stage a few days before, up north a ways. And that when he went to talk to Red about it, Red went for his gun and there was a shootout, but Red got away."

"This happened in town?"

"Yes, at Abbott's Livery, south end of town. The Abbotts also have a horse ranch a few miles away, so that's where he said Red would go. Seemed strange to me, when he said just to shoot him on sight. But I didn't argue, a'course."

"He never liked bein' spoke back to," I said. "We had our run-ins, back in the old days, me and Cal. Never did like the man."

Young Emmett swallowed the last of his coffee and nodded. "I already didn't trust Sheriff Pettygore, as you well know — not since that trouble last year at the orphanage. Please don't repeat that, of course, Georgina and Mary."

They both nodded an assurance, and Emmett went on with the story. He explained how he'd broken off from the posse and found tracks that led him to an abandoned farmhouse, which was where Red Abbott was hiding. And that, rather than just go in shooting, he called out to Red, told him he'd bring him in for trial alive.

Red hadn't believed him at first, but when he finally realized Emmett was alone, he'd called him in.

"He was in bad shape when I got there," said Emmett. "Had three bullets in him — two of those in his back. And he wasn't armed, Lyle."

"Did he explain it?"

"Red told me the Sheriff came to see him at the Livery — then just shot him, no warning at all."

"He'd expected some trouble?"

"Said he'd been warned. Said Sheriff Pettygore acted strange, then suddenly went for his Colt — Red leaped forward and punched him as he fired, but he'd took one low in the belly. He kicked the Sheriff in the face, ran out the back and jumped onto a horse he always kept saddled and waiting. Pettygore fired at him as he hightailed it, and Red took two in the back. Not deep, those — it was the first shot that did all the damage. I'm telling you, Lyle — there's a lot more to this than we know. But I'm sure glad you're here."

CHAPTER 5
"HE WAS GUTSHOT AND LOCO
WITH FEVER..."

I looked around the table. As always, Georgina was quiet, strong and thoughtful as we worked things out. Mary also kept quiet and listened, her eyes burning with desire for justice. And Deputy Emmett Slaughter, he was as good a young feller as ever pinned on a badge.

We were all in this together, and would follow it through to its end.

I looked into Emmett's tired eyes and said, "What happened when you found Red?"

"By then his belly was all swollen up and his fever was bad. We both knew he was dying, and he begged me to kill him quick and clean."

"But you couldn't."

Deputy Emmett Slaughter looked across to where his children were playing, and he sighed a deep one. "He was suffering terribly, Lyle. I offered to give him my six-gun and let him do it himself. But he told me he had to explain something first."

"And he told you he'd been there when Mary's parents were killed?"

We all looked at Mary then, but she raised her head high, and in a strong voice she said, "Please go on, Mister Deputy Emmett. I *must* find out the truth."

"Yes," Emmett said. "I know, Mary. Red was there when it happened, said it was a terrible shock. And he wanted me to know he didn't do it. Kept saying, *'No matter what they tell you, it weren't me or my brothers. We don't attend church, but we're God-fearing people, and my Ma never raised killers. Don't let her believe it, whatever they say. And we never killed my Pa neither.'* Red said a lot of other things too, he was speaking so fast with his words all coming out garbled. Some of it made no sense at all."

"But he gave you the name of the killer. Jesse Gillespie."

Emmett took off his hat, ran a hand through his hair, sighed again. "Yes, Lyle, that's the only name he gave before he died. And also, that Gillespie killed Red's father."

"A right dangerous feller, he sounds."

"Could be," Emmett replied. "Problem is, I cannot find any such man."

"You've searched all local records?"

"Local and more. Thing is though, I've had to be careful. Last thing Red said was *'Don't trust the Sheriff.'* I don't know anything for certain, but I can tell you this — Cal Pettygore seemed mighty keen to know whether Red talked when I found him. *Too* keen, if you know what I mean."

"You tell Pettygore anything?"

"I told him Red was on his last legs when I found him. And that the only thing Red said, was to tell his mother he loved her — then he died right away."

"So you've had to search the records without the Sheriff knowing you was looking into it?"

"That's the size and shape of it, Lyle," he said. "I wrote my old man and asked for his help — that made things a lot easier. He's friends with the Federal Marshal where he lives in Pittsburgh. The Marshal doesn't get involved, but he let Pa access the records one night at the courthouse."

"*That's* why the letter you sent had a Pittsburgh postmark on it," Georgina said, and he nodded. "It was driving me crazy."

"That was sharp thinking," I told him, "after your previous letter to me got *somehow* intercepted."

He screwed up his face in disgust. "Pettygore, without doubt."

"So did your Pa find anything useful?"

"He found records of only five people named Jesse Gillespie, including those with alternative spellings — J. E. S. S. I. E can be used for men too, and not only women. Of the five, one died in the war fifteen years back, one sailed for England soon after, and the other is ninety years old, and has never left Boston. And the two females are both children."

"Hmmm, it's a stumper," I said, as young Jeanie Slaughter brought out an apple pie as big as my head.

"That smells *mighty* fine, Ma'am," I said, as she cut it into generous slices.

"Cinnamon!" said Mary, and the women all shared a smile, as Emmett went on.

"Red said a lot of things in that few minutes, but at least half didn't make sense. Like I said, he was gutshot and loco with fever."

"Don't suppose you took any notes?"

"Soon as he died I took out my pencil," the young Deputy said. "Give me a moment, I'll go get the notes. I doubt they'll help, I've been through them *quite* a few times."

We all of us studied them notes, and by the time we was done we knew less than we had when we started.

Problem was, men say *all* sorts of things in the final throes of their dying. He had gone on and on of his love and respect for his mother — nothing strange about that. Devoted to her he was, by all accounts.

He had spoken of bribes and of Sheriffs, he had mentioned walnuts and horses, he had said that it weren't his Pa's fault, and not his brothers' neither.

"His brothers were there when it happened?"

"No, Lyle, I don't believe so, though I cannot be certain. Red had the delirium of death on him. Kept going on about horses. 'The mare! The mare!' Over and over. 'What mare,' I'd ask him. And he'd say, 'Our mare, a' course.' The mare he'd escaped from the Sheriff on was a pretty nice horse, so I guess he *was* quite attached to her."

"Like Dewdrop and me," Mary said. "You can understand *that,* can't you, Father?"

I turned to look at Horse, who was trying to pull down the fence I'd tied him up to, so he could go eat all Jeanie

Slaughter's flowers. I shook my head slowly, picked Emmett's notes up off the table and put on my glasses, to look at 'em proper this time.

"What's this scribbled up the side of it here?"

Young Deputy Emmett cocked his head sideways and squinted some at it. "Sorry, I should write neater. That just says *Pa done the dying. Big money. Jesse Gillespie.* That's how he put it. He was just about gone by then, Lyle."

"So we believe this Gillespie — or whatever his real name is — killed three people then. When did Red's father die?"

"Two days after the Wilsons."

"That murder investigated?"

"No," he said, shaking his head, slow and deliberate. "Record states that Red and his brothers saw it happen, down at the Livery, late in the night. He was cleaning his rifle, they reckoned."

We exchanged a meaningful glance.

"And the mother?"

"Sheriff told me to stay right away from her. Said she'd been through enough, and he'd handle it himself. She doesn't come into town much. I've never seen the woman, wouldn't know what she looked like."

"Surely you seen her at Red's funeral?"

"Sheriff forbade me from going."

"That don't make sense."

"None of it does," Emmett said, smiling at his wife as she placed a fork in his hand and nodded at the pie we'd been ignoring. Then he turned back toward me and said, "We'll go to the Abbott ranch tomorrow. If the Sheriff finds out, I'll tell him to fire me — and that if he does, I'll go up against him at next month's election."

"That's the way, son," I said with a nod of approval, and took up my fork. "Now let's sample this fine apple pie before it goes cold."

CHAPTER 6
YOUNG'UN

By the time we left Emmett Slaughter's, Mary was feeling the effects of long travel, and maybe some conflicting emotions as well.

It could not be easy, all this talk of her parents' murders.

We had planned to call in at the orphanage before going back to our hotel room, but Georgina suggested we put it off for a day or two. Blamed her *own* tiredness, she did — but I knew she had done it for Mary's sake.

One thing at a time.

We went back to town, and I helped young Roy Grimm to feed and water the horses, while my girls headed to the hotel for a well-deserved rest.

A train had come in from Sidney by then, and already there was some real nice horseflesh about, and Roy's stables were full as an egg with two yolks.

"That big gelding won at Sidney yesterday," Roy told me, pointing out a tall flashy bay in the stable next to Horse's. "Not the cup race, but a hundred dollar purse anyway. Trainer said he got odds of ten to one, made himself a passel of money from the bets. Over two-thousand he reckoned."

"Good work if you can get it," I replied, before thanking Roy for his trouble and slipping him a good tip. Never seemed right to me how Roy done all the work here, but only earned a small wage, while the feller who owned the place sat on his rump and scooped up all the profits for himself.

If Roy had his own place, every dang customer he has would go with him. Might should talk to him about that before we leave Cheyenne. Most especially now that he's married, he could use extra income.

I went back to the hotel, and looked through the window into the foyer. First thing I noticed was another one a'them signs, this one painted right on the wall, writ up in big foot-high letters.

ALL GUNS MUST BE HANDED IN.

Then in smaller letters underneath, it said:

Either Here Or At Sheriff's Office.
No Exceptions.

In theory, I quite *like* this rule for towns. Problem is, the bad fellers is the ones who'll ignore it — and then we got troubles aplenty, and less ways to fix 'em.

Well, at least now I can hand Gertrude in here, and not have to see that skunk Sheriff Cal Pettygore.

I strode across to the counter.

The desk clerk was a skinny, freckle-faced feller who'd worked in this hotel for years. He had always been in a hurry, one a'them scurrying types who tended to startle the horses until they got used to him.

Nice kid, I just wished he'd slow down and relax some. But some fellers is just naturally like that, and I guess you can't blame 'em for being however they are. Just trying to please folks I guess, and get lotsa work done in no time at all.

I never *could* remember his name, but anyway, he was the one who'd delivered the letter a year ago — *the letter telling me Bid had been murdered.*

If I ain't already told you that story, Bid was my lifelong best friend, and was married to Georgina for just about forty years, before me and her got hitched up. I had always loved her, a'course — but Bid scooped her up first, and you can't blame a friend for being smarter and faster when it matters.

Anyway, when I walked across the foyer and seen the young feller just now, I got some sort of a shock. Had to lean on the counter to save myself falling down.

Strange how a body reacts — soon as I seen his freckly face I felt a big damn hole in my chest, and it brought the bad news right back, just as fresh and hard and jagged as the moment I first read the letter.

The freckle-faced pencil-neck looked up from his paperwork and said, "You alright, Mister Frakes? I mean, no offense, but you look sorta—"

"I'm fine, young'un," I said, brushing some imaginary

dirt off the counter. "I see you got a well-deserved promotion since last I was here."

"Yes sir, thank you sir, I did. I'm the manager now, if you can believe it. Although I must say, Mister Frakes, you've been calling me *young'un* for quite a few years now, and I turned thirty-three just last month."

"Happy birthday, young'un," I told him. "I named a foal after you two weeks ago. It's a filly, but a good-lookin' type, and sorta freckled how you are. What room am I in?"

He reached around behind him and took a key from the pigeon-hole, handed it to me and said, "Room sixteen, Mister Frakes, sir. Your new wife ... that is, I'm sorry, sir, that was impertinent, I'll start again if that's alright. Your wife and child are up there resting, sir, is what I wanted to tell you. And may I say, *congratulations!*"

"Thanks, I guess. What *is* your name anyway, son? I'm tryin' to learn one each year — last year it was Roy Grimm, reckon this year I'll learn yours."

"Oh, thank you, sir," he said, his face breaking into a big toothy smile that made him look like a gopher. "He married my sister, you know. Roy, I mean. I like him a lot. Oh, and my name is Johnathon Quirk, sir. Most folks just call me John though. And thank you for naming the horse after me — even though it's a filly, it's still quite an honor."

"Glad you took it that way. Not everyone would."

"But I did wonder, Mister Frakes, sir — how did you name it after me, when you didn't know what my name was?"

"Called the foal *Young'Un,* a'course. Fine name, and she does look quite like you." I took a good look at him and rubbed at my beard some, as I cast my mind back through the years. "Don't guess you're related to *Randall* Quirk, are you? I had cause to arrest a man of that name several times. Not a *bad* feller, but he had a outsize fondness for startin' up drinkin', and no fondness for stoppin' at *all* once he got himself started. He'd just keep drinkin' til he fell down, or somebody knocked him down because he deserved it. Ol' Randall woulda got in less trouble if the drink didn't make his gums flap so quick. Town drunk down in Snaggle Rock, Texas, ol' Randall was. Prosperous place, now I think on it — as we had *two* town drunks. Naw," I said, looking into his overclear eyes, "you wouldn't be nohow related, sober feller like you."

"Yes, well," young Johnathon said, them eyes a'his darting every which way as he made sure no one else would hear him. "I know him as *Uncle* Randall, and my father tells me he's not *quite* so badly behaved now. Lives down in Denver, and I last saw him a little over five years ago, on his sixtieth birthday. Uncle Randall told us that day that he planned to live a sober life, and only drink on his birthday from that auspicious day forward."

"Can't imagine that of ol' Randall. Did he stick to it long, do you know?"

"Well, Father wrote me just last week — and according to his calculations, Uncle Randall is about to celebrate his two-thousandth birthday."

"Well, you tell him to have one for me, and another for his ol' drinkin' partner, Sourdough Dick. And tell him to make mine a brandy — I recall it being his favorite when he was cashed up."

CHAPTER 7
TEN-GAUGE

W hen I went up to our hotel room, Georgina
was indeed taking an afternoon nap, but
Mary wanted to talk.

Seemed she was worried about what had happened
when them foolish youngsters attempted to rob us on the
train.

"You done good, Mary," I told her.

"But I missed." She sounded mighty dejected about it.

"You done what was needed," I explained. "I reckon
you sensed they was kids, just as I did. And I reckon you
missed him on purpose. You hit targets nine outta ten,
whenever we practice. And you signaled just right."

"I would not have fired at all, only he waved his gun in
your direction. And you're right, Father, of course. I was *so*
afraid I might kill him. I switched my aim at the last
minute, so my bullet went over his shoulder and out
through the doorway."

"See? It went where you aimed. Don't you worry none,

child — your aim will be true if ever one of us is in danger. We ain't murderers, Mary. Good people only kill when we have to, but then we don't hesitate. You done good. You'll be just fine."

I told her I'd be going out to see Red Abbott's mother early next morning without her. Told her she should take her mother shopping instead.

The child tried to argue at first. But she gave it up quick enough when I took out a hundred dollars and told her they had to spend every penny before I got back, or I'd waste it on gambling.

We all had hot baths before eating early that evening, then we turned in to catch up on sleep.

Sure was nice to sleep in a bed that weren't rattling and bumping and creaking like the one on the train did.

I woke at 5.30 and dressed, collected Gertrude from the feller on night duty, then walked up the street to the Livery in relative darkness.

Unlike what we'd gotten used to back in Santa Monica, there was no morning fog, no sound of waves breaking, no sea breeze to buffet a man as he started his day.

No taste of salt in the air — I miss that, now it ain't there.

Weren't all bad, a'course — instead of all that, there was clear air and stillness, the quiet of the town at this hour a pleasant reminder of why I had chosen to live around these parts some years back.

Roy Grimm was already up and about when I walked in through the doors. He had a few lamps burning to light the place up, and there are few smells more pleasant than a well-run Livery in the early part of the morning.

Despite Roy's bad leg being stiff and painful at this time of day, he greeted me happily and asked if I'd be attending the horse race the following weekend.

"Reckon Georgina and Mary will drag me along," I said. "And if they don't drag me, I'll drag them. Always good fun, a horse race. I'll be there, young Roy, with a handful of gambling money."

"Good," he replied. "My wife's away visiting her mother, but I'm hoping she'll be back in time. If she is, we might share a picnic, so you and your family can meet her."

"Look forward to it," I said. "Turns out I knew her Uncle some years back. Young Johnathon caught me up on all that."

Roy laughed it up and said, "Don't you worry, Mister Frakes. My Cindy's a woman of more-or-less sober habits. Don't get me wrong, she's no Temperance[1] woman, but she ain't like some a'her kin. Why, I met her Uncle Randall one time, and he drank enough for a whole army all by himself."

I saddled Horse for the trip out to the Abbott Ranch, drank a cup of Roy's coffee then left the Livery by the back lane at five after six.

Weren't the best, young Roy's coffee. I'd best give him some pointers sometime. If he ever makes that for his wife he could end up divorced.

Ordinary circumstances, me and Deputy Emmett woulda met up in town and rode out together. But what with us being suspicious of Sheriff Cal Pettygore, we had decided the less me and Emmett was seen in town together the better.

So I left by the back lane and went south a ways in case someone was watching. Then I turned a couple of lefts and took a back street to meet up with young Slaughter at his place. The Abbott Ranch was six miles north-east of town, so we had to go past Emmett's anyway — and a'course, after working all night, he needed some breakfast.

I arrived just a few minutes after he did, and when his good wife Jeanie put a steaming plate of ham and eggs on the table before me, along with a big china cup of her excellent coffee, well, it woulda been downright rude to refuse it.

A lot of women woulda complained about their husbands going out to investigate killings on their own time, way we was about to. Not Jeanie — she knows that good man a'hers ain't in the job only for money. Fine woman. Just fine.

By the time Jeanie waved us goodbye, it was already six-thirty, and the sun was already yawning, and threatening to wake. As we took the road to the north-east, a few wagons came into view on their way into town, each driver rugged up against the cold, and nodding a friendly one as they went by us.

When we rode past the orphanage where Mary used to live, I was happy to see there weren't no children working the fields, way there woulda been before I killed that skunk August Benson who used to run the place. Emmett told me Mavis Benson was doing a fine job of looking after the children now, and they was all getting proper schooling, in addition to learning useful life skills a few hours a day.

As is my usual practice, I held Horse to a walking pace for the most part as we headed out to the Abbott place.

Never know when you might need to gallop — so always best to save up your horse for the moment you'll need him.

It was a pleasant ride, and I sure enjoyed the company. With time to more thoroughly discuss things, young Emmett Slaughter went into more detail of his investigations. He had not shirked his task. There wasn't a thing I could think of that he hadn't done, besides speaking to the Abbotts — which we was about to start doing today.

And while we would speak with Red's brothers at *some* point, we had good reason to begin with their mother — Emmett had the feeling the brothers were mixed up in something, but the mother might not be.

Emmett spoke Red's exact words now, as we discussed it — *'No matter what they tell you, it weren't me or my brothers. We're God-fearing people, and my Ma never raised killers. Don't let her believe it, whatever they say. And we never killed my Pa neither.'*

"*Don't let her believe it,*" I repeated, and pondered it some. "There was threats made to Red, by the sounds. Threats that SOMEONE would tell his mother that HE killed the Wilsons, *and* killed his own Pa."

"Well, I hope we learn *something,* this is the Abbott place here," Emmett said, as he reined his horse to a stop outside a particularly fine ranch and took out his pocket watch. He opened the watch, cupped a hand over it to combat the glare, and closed one eye to look at the time. "Seven-forty-five."

"Don't see no one about," I said.

"She'll be here alright. Way rumor has it, Red's funeral was the only time she's left the place since burying her husband two years back." Emmett carefully closed the watch and put it away. "They say she'd become a recluse, even before that. Might as well ride in and see if she's willing to talk."

As we rode toward the houses, I took it all in. It was what Mary refers to as an *idyllic spot.*

I don't know what bein' idle has to do it with it — it takes a whole lotta work to make a place this good, and a whole lotta money as well.

What a place.

Perfect silence, except for the sounds of good horses cropping good grass — and birds singing too, at this hour.

A bubbling creek running through it was just the beginnings of what made it special. Beside that creek stood a tall windmill — and by the lush green of the pastures, it was clear that the whole place could be watered as much as they wanted. There was two nice log cabins, an oversize barn painted white, and a whole lotta quality fencing with the sorta horses that matched it.

Place looks like a proper thoroughbred stud, like you'd see in Kentucky.

"Business is good by the looks," I said.

"Sure looks that way," Emmett replied.

That's when a large woman stepped out onto the porch of the nearer cabin, and proceeded to blow the peaceful silence to hell with a big ten-gauge shotgun.

---

1. TEMPERANCE: The history of the Temperance Movement is often misunderstood these modern times. It was not for total abstinence from alcohol, but against OVERINDULGENCE of hard spirits, due to the moral, economical and medical effects. Still, in some places this was taken to extremes, which often led to violence against Temperance members.

CHAPTER 8

"YOU'RE THE DAMN SKUNK
KILLED MY BOY..."

"S tate your business," the huge woman cried from the porch as she reloaded. "Next shots goes through your fat empty heads."

Thing was, we was still seventy yards off, and there weren't no way that big scattergun was gonna do us no damage from that far away.

Still, you had to respect her — she had made herself clear.

We stopped where we were and Emmett called out, "I'm Deputy Emmett Slaughter of Cheyenne, Ma'am. I was hoping to speak to you about—"

"You're the damn skunk killed my boy," she cried out. "Sure, ride on in. This gun a'mine feels like talkin' to *you,* real personal-like."

Emmett glanced at me a moment and took a big breath before speaking again. "Ma'am, please," he called to her, top of his lungs. "If that's what you were told, you were lied to. But I *was* with Red when he died."

"A'course you was there, you could not have killed him from elsewhere!"

"Ma'am, please. There's more to all this than the Sheriff's letting on. I don't believe Red robbed any stagecoach at all. Also, he gave me a message to give you."

"That's been weeks now since you killed him. Why ain't you come out here already with this message, so-called? And why would I trust my son's killer? You come any closer I'll blow you to bits."

Emmett turned to me, shrugged his shoulders.

"Let me try," I said.

He took off his hat, ran his fingers through his hair, and nodded a deliberate one. "Can't do any worse than I did. I should have come out here sooner."

"Missus Abbott," I called. "I ain't a lawman no more, but I got wide experience in that field, and it's my strong belief your son and your husband was murdered by some real bad skunks."

"My husband died cleaning his gun," she shouted. "Get on your way, 'fore I lose what's left a'my temper and fill you with holes."

"All due respect, but did that gun-cleanin' story seem likely to you, Ma'am? All reports, your husband weren't no sorta fool. That story's corral dust[1], and I reckon you know it. We just wanna talk, Ma'am, you can keep hold a'the gun, and we'll lay ours down if you like. Please, Missus Abbott, this is important. I don't want no more a'your sons killed, and that there's the truth of it."

She stayed quiet a few moments, and I figured she

weren't gonna answer. But then she called out, "Who are you, and why are you here?"

I like it when someone gets to the point, so I quickly answered in kind.

"My name's Lyle Frakes. I came to Cheyenne to solve the murder of—"

"Why didn't you say so in the first place?" she called. "Lyle Frakes is welcome at the Abbott place anytime. You vouch for this tenderfoot Deputy you brung along with you? And did he kill my boy or he didn't? You tell me straight, Frakes."

"I vouch for the tenderfoot — he's a good honest lawman, and they's in short supply around these parts, that much I do know."

"So it wasn't him killed my Redmond?"

"It was Sheriff Cal Pettygore killed your son, and it should say so in the records, unless they's been altered unlawfully. We all good to come talk now?"

"Ride on in," she called. "But I warn you, I know Frakes by sight. And if you ain't him, I'll blow you boys both to hell afore you can spit."

---

1. CORRAL DUST: Tall tales or lies — and just as easy to choke on as real corral dust kicked up by horses

CHAPTER 9
BAD DUST & POLLENS

L ucky for us, I still looked enough like myself to pass muster, despite it being ten years since Delvene Abbott had seen me.

While we approached, she retreated inside, watched us the whole time from the doorway, with the door three-parts closed. All we could see was them two gaping barrels, rock-steady and pointed right at us.

No matter how many times you stare down a scattergun, there's a horror about it you never get comfortable with.

"You're older'n'uglier than when I last seen you," she said when she opened the door and laid down the Greener. "But you're Frakes alright, and that's the same horse you was mounted on ten years ago. Horse was young then, a'course, but you was already old. Well, come on in, we'll have coffee. And make sure to wipe your damn boots."

Turned out I had met these Abbotts before, down in Texas.

They had owned very little back then, and all three of

their horses had been stolen by Mexican rustlers. I was out of my own jurisdiction, but I had been tracking those horse-thieves for over a week, and I weren't about to let some invisible line stop me from doing what was right.

They had stolen from friends of mine too — and I got a special sorta dislike for horse thieves. Just ain't fair to the horses.

When I caught up to the skunks, it was only two men, not a gang, and I took them in without spilling one drop of blood — mine *or* theirs. Their own fault it was, getting too greedy. Two men ain't nearly enough for seventy horses, and they kept losing some then rounding them back up. Slowed 'em down, made 'em easy to catch.

Upshot was, I got a list of the brands, and returned the right horses to Delvene Abbott and her husband — plus gave 'em one extra, unbranded, that no one reported. *Well, I could see they was struggling.*

I remembered the woman once she explained it. And despite her opinion of me having got older and uglier, I never returned the same compliment — though it woulda been truthful, and then some.

Even back then, she was possessed of such beauty as woulda scared off a bear, even one who had always been unlucky in love, and consequently weren't picky. But in the ten years since then, she had clearly not missed no meals, and had growed at a most alarming rate. Yes, Delvene Abbott was now a giant-size tree-stump of a woman, and undoubtedly would measure much longer wide-ways than what she would tall-ways.

But that ain't the true measure of a woman, and barely

don't count for nothin' in the great scheme of things. More important by far, she was one a'them type who can drink and swear and fight like a man — and yet still somehow be soft and caring and loving with their own kin.

And it being just weeks since she'd lost Red — and also, he was her youngest — she had cause to wipe tears from her eyes several times while we spoke.

I mean, she growled when she wiped at her eyes, and swore it was a dose of the hay-fever sorely afflicting her — *"Bad dust and pollens, this time a'year..."* — but her bottom lip wobbled too, and we looked away every time so she wouldn't be embarrassed.

After she brought us coffee she looked me in the eye and said, "Why would my own boys lie to me? About their Pa's death, that two years back, I mean. They can be wild, but they always been mostly good boys."

"We're looking into that, Ma'am," I told her.

"If you call me Ma'am one more time," she said, "I'll be famous all over as the woman who killed Lyle Frakes with only one punch. You best call me Delvene, so as we can stay friends."

And she laughed so hard it wobbled her chins like a great big strawberry jelly, before slapping my back so hard it just about knocked me off a'my chair.

CHAPTER 10
GETTIN' SOFT, ME, IN MY DOTAGE...

Y oung Emmett told her of Red's final moments, and I must say, he done a fine job of a delicate thing.

Ain't easy, telling a mother of how her boy went to his final rest — but the Deputy softened the blow some, and made sure she knew just how much Red respected and loved her.

He didn't push the woman at all, but we watched her reactions to everything he told her, all the things Red had said.

Clear enough, she knew nothing of Jesse Gillespie, or anymuch else for that matter. When we asked, she said that she had little contact with anyone these days — had not even attended horse-races for maybe five years now, for she'd lost interest in it.

"I do love the horses," she said. "But I don't like the racing anymore."

She did wonder why Emmett had not attended Red's

burial — she said she'd have noticed a handsome young feller like him, even though there was more than sixty folks in attendance. Emmett told her the truth — that Sheriff Cal Pettygore had told him he wasn't to go, or to have any contact whatsoever with her, or with Red's brothers neither.

She looked hard into his eyes then, said, "And it was Pettygore fired the shot that killed Redmond?"

"Yes, Ma'am. Missus Abbott. Delvene. According to Red, that's who shot him. Strange thing is, Sheriff Pettygore told me he went to the Livery to speak to Red about a stage robbery. And he said Red went for his gun, so he shot him, then Red overpowered him and rode off."

"Red never shot so much as a rabbit in his whole life. Never liked guns at all. I'd sooner believe the boy grew wings and flew, than shot someone with a gun."

"He did not have one on him, Missus Abbott, when I found him. No powder on his hands neither. Other thing strange, the Sheriff had every one of us Deputies searching, and told us to shoot Red on sight. Said he was loco and dangerous. That made no sense at all — it's not normal procedure, and Pettygore never instructed us that way before. There's something big happening here, and your son got himself in the middle of it somehow. Any ideas on what it might be?"

She pondered some on it, sadly shaking her head, but she didn't know. She searched Emmett's face and then mine, then said, "You believe his father was murdered by this Jesse Gillespie, and those other folk was killed by him too."

"Yes, Ma'am," Emmett told her. "Seems to us it's related to *why* Red was killed, but we cannot find any clues as to what it might be. And we cannot find Jesse Gillespie — it's not the man's *real* name anyway, whoever he is."

I laid a firm hand on the brave woman's shoulder. "Delvene, listen," I said. "It ain't my true nature to stick my beak in people's business — but a certain degree of stickybeakin' is sometimes required to bring bad men to justice."

"Whatever it is, ask away," she said, rubbing some a'them bad dusts and pollens outta her eyes. "Justice, that's all I want. And for my other boys to be safe. Tell me straight, Frakes, are they too in danger?"

"We don't know, Delvene, not for certain. But usually, when there's killings, it's about money. And we know you have the Livery in town, and it does pretty well. But this ranch a'yours ... I won't dance it around it, Delvene, there's some serious money sunk into this place, and it didn't all come from that Livery."

"I can see why you'd think it," she said, nodding thoughtful and slow. "And I reckon you're right. But I promise you, Frakes, I got no idea about where our recent wealth come from. Henry was a good man, but he didn't like me asking questions related to money. By the way, you know that extra horse you gifted to us, when you brung ours home back in sixty-eight?"

"A big bay colt, weren't he? High-stepper, spirited beast, just a yearling back then."

"That's him," she replied, going back to the stove to get us all some more coffee. "You got a good memory, Frakes."

"For horses I do, but not people — at least lately, that's been the case." Then I admitted, "I didn't recognize your name when I heard it, for instance, but knew you once I seen you close up."

"Age'll get us all thusly," she said, and it weren't an insult, so I didn't mind none. "That horse made a real difference to our fortunes, Frakes. He was fast, that big feller — we still got him, you know, our best stallion. He's the horse got us mixed up with racing, and he won pretty often. Nothin' big, mind, but we traveled the circuit once he turned three. He won as much as he lost for two years, and the bets we made bought us this place, and got us our start."

"But this place is ... well, it's more than a start, ain't it, Delvene?"

I blew the steam off my coffee and tried it, but it was too hot yet to drink. *Gettin' soft, me, in my dotage.*

"My Henry was an honest man, Frakes. *At his core, anyway.* But the racing game attracts all sorts — some's honest, some's not."

"I got a friend or two in it," I told her, "and I reckon you're right, it averages out."

"Henry got mixed up in *something,* but he never told me. All I know is, he'd go away a few weeks, and when he'd get back he'd have horses *and* extra money than what he had left with."

"And your boys?"

She took a big mouthful a'coffee like as if it was more-or-less cold, and then she went on. "Sometimes he'd take Redmond with him, sometimes Clarence, sometimes

Benjamin." She smiled a wry one and added, "They hate when I use their full names, but I often do. I'm proud a'them boys."

"By all accounts, you should be," I told her.

But the thing about all that was, her boys was involved in this up to their ears — and while I respected Delvene, them boys a'hers might well be killers, no matter who said what, or when.

I took a big gulp of my coffee and burned my dang tongue as she spoke up again.

"I never *really* believed Henry died from cleaning his gun. But my boys said they seen it, and I guess I just went along with it. I always sensed *something* was happening, ever since Henry's first trip to the East to buy horses three years back. That's when the money began to roll in, you see?" She sighed a deep one, shook her head slowly, went on. "I'll talk to my boys — don't *you* try it, they'll clam right up — and if I get somewhere I'll let you know. But for now, I ain't got nothin' for you."

"One last thing, Delvene," I said as I got to my feet. "Did you know the folks who were murdered two days before your husband? The Wilsons. I adopted their daughter, and that's why we came — because Red wanted all that put right. At least, that's what he told my young friend here."

"I heard tell about them poor folks," she said, and she frowned. "But not til after Henry was dead, so I had my own problems and upsets. I'm sorry, but I didn't know them. I keep to myself, pretty much. Like to stay home, work with the horses, read my bible and such."

"Don't go to church?"

"Don't like churches *or* preachers — but I do like my time with the Good Book. Feel free to come back anytime, Frakes. You too, young Deputy. And I thank you for letting me know what my Redmond said at the end. Means a lot to a mother."

"We'll do what Red hoped we would," I said, shaking her hand at the door as she seen us out. "Please don't say anything to your boys that might let the Sheriff know we suspect *him*. And I promise, Delvene, we'll get to the bottom of these murders, or my name ain't Lyle Frakes."

CHAPTER 11

IF THERE'S ONE THING I HATE...

After leaving Emmett Slaughter to catch up on some sleep, I made my way back into town and went straight to the Livery.

While I attended to Horse I spoke briefly with Roy of his plans for the future, pointing out that he was the one doing all a'the work at this Livery, and gettin' almost none a'the money.

He said he'd been thinking about it, and that his new wife Cindy had spoke to him too on the subject, and they had made a few plans.

"Cindy works stitching leather right now — she makes fine reins and bridles and such like — but the couple she works for have plans to move back to Chicago early next year. That's why Cindy's down in Denver right now — not just to *visit* her parents, but to see if they might lend us money to start renting the building the saddlery's in."

"That the one over on Love Street?"

"That's it alright, Mister Frakes, right on the edge of town but still close enough in to be part a'things."

"Got a big barn out back, ain't it?" I said, and he nodded. "Big enough for some stables, that barn, and what? An acre or so that goes with it."

"Yessir, almost two acres. Even got a good well there for water, and an upstairs to live in."

"Sounds a prime opportunity, young Roy. When will you know?"

"Cindy hopes to be back on Thursday, if her mother's feeling better," Roy said, as I left Horse's stall after one final scratch of his ears. "The woman took ill a few days back, but it's hopefully nothing serious. Anyway, Cindy'll let me know when she returns. Fingers crossed, Mister Frakes — but I ain't got my hopes up. They ain't got much to spare, Cindy's folks, that's why she moved up here in the first place."

When I picked up Gertrude to leave, Roy told me I could leave her right there if I wanted, and he'd hide her away in a secret spot he had built for that very purpose. He said the rules about guns had been somewhat relaxed, and Hotels and Liveries both was included as places folks could leave guns.

"Makes perfect sense," I said. "There's hope for this town yet, I reckon."

We said our goodbyes and I went for a quiet brandy at the nearest saloon. Law of averages told me I wouldn't have trouble there this time — it was the same place I'd got into a fight when last I'd been here a year ago. *Woke up in the jailhouse that time.*

Given its close proximity to the Sheriff's Office, I figured the drinkers inside should be well behaved. Besides which, it was a Monday — that must stand for something.

Quietest day, drinking-wise, I had always noticed — except for the Sabbath, some places.

I therefore expected to find just a few quiet souls, slowly bending an elbow and perhaps reminiscing about the old days, before Cheyenne became the busy town it is today.

Well a'course, I hadn't reckoned on an influx of tourists, due to the upcoming horse-race and big town parade.

I looked in through the window — just to see if that skunk Sheriff Cal Pettygore was inside. If he was, I'd position myself in a way I could hear him, but where I'd not get myself noticed.

Oh, he'd know I was in town. But he had no reason to think nothing of it. Then again, by now he would know I'd adopted Mary — and if he knew *anything* about the murder of Mary's parents, he would perhaps be suspicious of why I was here.

Either way, the saloon that is nearest the hoosegow is often a good place to find information, big town like Cheyenne.

Worth investing an hour to try — and if I had to drink two small brandies, well, that was a price I would just have to pay.

Pettygore weren't to be seen, and I didn't see no other lawmen inside. I walked in through the batwings, and several of the drinkers looked my way, as a slight hush came over the place, then some murmurs.

Same as most other times I walk into a place. Always a few folks who knows who I am, around these parts.

But pretty much right away, it went back to how it was just before I walked in. Sure was busy in there though.

I went to the bar, got a brandy. *Top shelf, a'course — might's well enjoy my bad habits.*

There weren't nowhere to sit, so I found a quiet wall to lean on in a back corner. Pretty good spot — I could see everyone in the place, and also the door.

I settled myself in to watch and to listen, and perhaps glean some new information.

It's always an interesting mix, when some sorta traveling circus comes to a town. And horse-racing, that's a circus with more of a wide-ranging mix than most others.

Them that wears fancy suits, and them that wears rags, just for starters.

The fellers always lookin' to gull you, and them who work daylight to dusk, never shirking a task in the care of the horses.

And of course, the greatest divide is that between the honest man, and he who is less so — though I will say, the former is generally in short supply when the big money men come to town.

Still, not every man in a suit is dishonest — just as not every man with a gun is looking to use it for nefarious purpose.

This being the fanciest of the Cheyenne saloons — *big chandelier, thousand-dollar mirror, and girls with expensive-looking smiles* — it was filled up today with that type a'man who wears tailor-made suits, for the most part.

Thing is though, that sort rarely go nowhere without *some* protection — and by that I mean men with guns. *Men who know how to use 'em.* A'course, here in Cheyenne with their fancy new gun laws, them guns would be small and well-hid — just like Wilma, my tiny Remington Rider, right here inside my coat pocket.

Still, in this *particular* saloon, even them gun-toting types is well-dressed, and all looking mighty respectable.

I slowly savored my first drink, listening to the talk all around me, but I didn't hear nothing useful. It was all about the merits of jockeys, the styles each one employed, and whether or not some famous little feller from back East would turn up, as was rumored.

All them words I was hearing might as well have been spoken in Chickasaw, all the sense I made of 'em.

I headed for the bar and bought my second brandy, and while I was there I noticed a group of fellers vacating a table, other side of the room.

I made for the spot, hoping I might hear something useful from there — but failing that, at least I now had a seat to rest my tired bones on awhile as I listened.

I had no sooner placed my drink on the table, when a giant hand squeezed my shoulder and a booming great voice said, "Move on, old-timer, this table's taken."

I have never liked being touched by a stranger, and the disrespect in his voice also rankled me some — and dammit, if there's one thing I hate, it's bein' called OLD.

CHAPTER 12
LITTLE WAYNE LOGAN

I looked in surprise at the bucket-sized hand, then turned to look at the man's face. Well, next surprise was, his face weren't there where it shoulda been — instead, what was there was a huge barrel chest.

The giant wore no jacket at all, only a much-too-tight shirt as a covering. Worse still, half a'the buttons was left all undone, like he *wanted* folks to see what he shoulda kept hidden away while he was in public.

Now, I ain't no dwarf, and am mostly unaccustomed to having to look upways when speaking to other men. Sure, maybe I have to look upways a *little* sometimes — but not usually more than an inch or two, which ain't hardly enough that I'd notice.

But this feller, he had to be six-foot-ten, and in addition to that mighty chest, he had upper arms that veritably rippled with muscle.

So a'course, I done what *any* sensible feller would do in that situation.

Well alright, you got me, I didn't...

But bear with me, I had my reasons for doing what I did next.

Instead of moving quietly along like most *clever* men would have, I said, "It just ain't polite to manhandle a stranger, and if your damn hand ain't gone by the time I count five, I'll teach you the lesson your own father should have, ya stinkin' great streak of wet cowdung."

Well, the whole place went awful quiet then, way such places do whenever such clear words are spoken. The big feller's eyes went wide at the insult, but instead of reacting the way I expected — which woulda been to throw a big, slow, wild punch — the feller's unhatted head spun about to look to a short, over-dressed, over-fed, over-fancy feller behind him, a feller who wore enough hat for three men, maybe more.

So that short fancy feller tilted his head back to see out from under his twenty-five gallon hat, and summed everything up. He looked from his man to me, and he licked his over-red lips like as if he had just spied a real tasty meal on his plate. Then looking back to his own man, he smiled a wicked tight smile and said, "Keep your hand right where it is, Logan. Allow the old fool to count — and when he reaches five, you shall teach *him* a lesson he'll never forget. That is to say, he'll learn from it *if* he survives."

Thing was, I had seen over-muscled fellers like this accompanying short, inadequate rich men twice before during my long career. And this feller showed all the same signs as them other two had — their necks was too thick and their forearms too slender to have built all them muscles from doin' anything useful.

They had built them huge muscles from lifting heavy anvils up and down or some such useless exercise — but fellers built like that have never done very much fighting or actual work.

Such muscles was all smoke and mirrors, would be my main meaning. And the improper balance of 'em makes the man mostly weak.

Still, this Logan was a biggun. So when he turned around and said in a great booming voice, "You heard Mister Lannigan, start counting, old man," I changed how I went about things.

"You do the count then, ya uglified bull-headed bird-brain," I said. "That's if ya *can* count to five, ya poor simpleton."

A sorta bellowing sound came outta him then, and there was mutterings in the background of how I would surely be killed — though I did hear one fella say, "Fifty on the old man if I get five to one," and someone took him up on the bet.

Then the outraged over-growed feller bent forward so his face was right down near mine, and called, "One!" before turning to smile at his boss.

"*FIVE,*" I yelled, landing a punch to his damn solar plexus that woulda brung a full-growed grizzly bear to its knees.

As the poor wheezing fool doubled over, I grabbed two good handfuls of his hair, jerked his massive head downways with all the force I could muster, and smashed my big right knee into his stupid face.

He kept trying, I'll give him that — but there ain't a man alive who can fight without breath, and that full-blooded right fist to his solar plexus had left him with no air inside him, and no way to get some.

He should not have bent forward to speak in that way, and left his belly wide open. No experienced fighter would be such a fool as to do so.

He grabbed a hold a'my shoulders with what strength he could, and made an attempt to go on, as his boss urged him to *"Kill the old fool, you big lump."*

Well, I won't lie, I *was* quite enjoying myself — but while ever he stayed on his feet, the thing wasn't settled. Them weak forearms a'his weren't no match for the strength of me drivin' up off a'my legs, and I smashed my right elbow against the side of his jaw, the effect of it being to make his eyes flutter, and his own legs to stagger as he tried to steady his bulk.

He stumbled a little, but stayed on his feet once again — so this time I hit him with the sweetest left hook I have thrown this past fifteen years.

His hands fell down by his sides, his knees buckled underneath him, and he fell — slow and heavy in the midst of a great booming silence — like a massive great redwood, he hit the floor with an echoing crash, and the only thing moving in that whole saloon was the dust-cloud that kicked up around him.

"Anyone else wish to dance?" I asked, looking around

me to see if I'd find any takers. No surprise when there weren't none.

Then I stared at the cowering feller who'd ordered the giant to give me a beating, and told him, "You might should learn better manners, you skeezy[1] little skunk. Next time I'll come after you too. Lannigan, weren't it? I won't forget. You best stay right outta my way."

Then I tipped the barman five dollars to make sure the giant got seen by a doctor, and drank down my brandy, one gulp, instead of enjoying it slowly.

"Ruined a nice quiet drink," I said to myself as I picked up my hat and began to walk out. "Still, it weren't all bad I guess. An old man *should* get some exercise, time to time. It's good for the spirit."

---

1. SKEEZY: Sleazy or sickly

CHAPTER 13
LIGHT OF MY LIFE

My girls had made the most of their day without me, and managed to buy small amounts of clothes, shoes, hats, perfumes and jewelry — all this under budget, they informed me, due to their superior bargaining skills, and the happy mood currently prevailing in the town of Cheyenne.

This mood was mostly due to the carnival atmosphere of the horse racing, which, though still several days away, was the talk of the town.

When I met them back in our hotel room, first thing Georgina said was, "Oh, Lyle, you're missing a button, whatever *have* you been up to? *And* you've been drinking!"

I considered explaining what happened, but my wife don't really approve of some types of enjoyments. So I just said, "Sorry, Princess, I got caught up on the batwings when I walked into the saloon. Musta lost the button then I guess. I'll go back and look for it *now* if you like — maybe have a second brandy while I'm at it."

"Hmmph," was the sound she made as she checked the state of my eyes. *"Already* had two, by the looks. You stay right here, I have spares, I'll sew one on tonight."

"Can't put nothin' past you," I said. "How went the shopping?"

Mary was keen to catch me up on all the news. Not only the news of their purchases, but all the rumors and such about horse-racing too.

Despite her complete lack of knowledge on the subject, and being of an age at which gambling should not be encouraged, she proceeded to regale me with the names of which horses were expected to win, and which others might prove to be interesting bets at long odds.

Well, she mighta knowed little about it, but she hadn't took but a day to learn most a' the jargon.

Georgina had obviously given up trying to keep the child off the subject of horses, and only rolled her eyes at each new mention of them, as we whiled away the afternoon in our comfortable room. They not only modeled all their new attire for me, but we also made plans for where we might go the next day, which would be Tuesday.

I told them a little of what Delvene Abbott had said, but left out the fact that the Abbotts were a horse-racing family. Having discussed it with Emmett as we returned, we'd decided to keep a few things to ourselves, so as not to risk Mary letting anything slip if she got talking to strangers roundabout town.

She ain't exactly a gossip, but she can be a little too trusting when she meets new people.

As they seemed keen to get involved in the carnival

atmosphere, I did suggest to Georgina and Mary that we might maybe get up before daybreak next morning and head on out to the racecourse, have a look at some horses as they went through their paces in the cool of the day.

"Oh, Father," said Mary, extravagantly rolling her eyes. *"Everyone* knows the best horses are to gallop on Wednesday, including the even money Cup favorite, *Light of My Life."*

"I'm the light a'your life, am I, girl? What a nice thing to say — I reckon you light mine up too."

Georgina managed to keep a straight face, but Mary fell for the bait, hook line and sinker.

"Oh, Father, surely you *must* know that Light of My Life is the name of a wonderful horse! Why, she won the Sidney Cup by four lengths just two days ago, easing down at the line!"

"Aw, that's sad alright," I said, managing a pretty convincing impression of sadness — not just with the tone of my voice but the slump of my body. "For a minute there, I thought maybe you actually liked me. You're as bad as that dang unfaithful old horse a'mine."

A'course, I had overacted my part, my acting skills being poor, and little Mary was onto me in a moment. She giggled that wonderful little-girl giggle she has, and ran headlong across the room toward me, leaping into my arms and commencing to slather my bearded old face with more kisses than I deserved.

"Well of *course* you light up my life, you funny old man," she said, still giggling for all she was worth. "And of course it goes without saying that Mother does too. But it does not change the fact that *Wednesday* is the day for the *smarties* to be at the track, so that's when *we* shall be there."

I placed her down on the floor, whereupon she retreated to her own bed, jumping backways onto it and landing in the middle with a greatly exaggerated spreading of her arms.

"Smarties now, are we?" I said. "Fine talk for a respectable child. You pick up on any more a'that horse-racing balderdash, one a'them trainers'll scoop you up for a jockey, and we won't never see you again."

The child's eyes lit up some at the idea, but her mother soon brought her back to the truth of it, when she pointed out that the jockeys only spend minutes riding, and a lotta time mucking out stalls, before digging huge holes to bury the stuff they collected.

"I have an idea then," she said, her little face positively gleeful. "Perhaps we could go pay a visit to dear Mrs Benson out at the orphanage tomorrow. She *was* my only real friend out there after all. And besides, Princess Mayblossom Gwendoline Winifred Regina Cordelia told me last night she wished to visit, as Mrs Benson was so kind as to let us both read her wonderful dictionary when last we were there."

Georgina gave me a quick nod of approval, so I rubbed my chin and tried to look thoughtful a moment before saying, "Since when did Princess Rugbottom start going by her full name again? I thought she was done with all that."

Mary consulted briefly with the doll — it was propped up beside her on her pillow, watching us with them beady button eyes. After much whispering in both directions, Mary told us the doll had put forward a deal.

"My wonderful doll will consent to being referred to by the short version of her name — *to wit, Princess Mayblossom* — for a period of seven days. She offers this deal in exchange for a one-hour visit with dear Mrs Benson."

"Well," I announced, after furiously deliberating with myself — a whole lotta whispers into my hand, which I then placed up by my ear for awhile — "As I *already* had plans to visit Mavis Benson tomorrow, I reckon that's a pretty fair deal. We'll ride out soon as we finish breakfast."

Danged if Princess Mussbuttons didn't fly right through the air and punch me square on the nose.

CHAPTER 14
RETURN TO THE ORPHANAGE

As planned, we rode out to the orphanage after a leisurely breakfast the very next morning.

It had rained some during the night, but not so much as to make the short trip unpleasant — and indeed, there are few smells more agreeable than the fragrance of slightly damp dirt, dug up and shifted around by the feet of good horses.

During the night I had wandered down to the jailhouse to discuss things with young Emmett Slaughter, and he'd promised to let Mavis Benson know to expect us sometime after eight, once the children were mostly in school.

We arrived at eight-thirty, and Mavis was already waiting out on the porch of the main building. She waved happily as soon as she saw us, and her posture made a striking contrast to that of the woman I'd met here a year ago — *before* I killed her husband, would be my main meaning.

Instead of the slouch so common in miserable folk, she was bolt upright now, her arms both waving extravagantly. And though it was too far to see, I knew she was smiling fit to warm hearts.

"Mary," she cried, running down the stairs as we came closer. "It's so lovely to see you. And Mister Frakes too, oh, I thank the dear Lord for you every night when I'm saying my prayers. What you did for us here made the lives of my charges a hundred times better than before! And this must be Mrs Frakes with you. It's so lovely to meet you."

We climbed down and tied Dewdrop and Gray to the rail, but I left Horse loose just in case.

I was nervous to be here, after what happened last year, I guess. Though the place looked and felt very different to what it had then.

First thing Mary done once she tied her horse to the rail was go straight to Mavis and hug her, before looking up into the woman's kind face and saying, "If not for you, I'd have done myself a bad mischief, Ma'am, when I lived here. And I know all the meanness I went through wasn't your fault. Your husband was a very bad man, and the beatings he gave turned some of the children mean too. Why, I'd take two-to-one odds they're all *much* kinder now — oh, please, tell me they are!"

"Oh, Mary," she said, her eyes filling with tears. "You always were such a wise one. Yes, you're right. Most of that mean behavior is gone, though it took a good while. And some of the older children moved out and found jobs, or moved to different cities and towns — I speak of the *worst* offenders, and I'm certain you know who I mean."

Well, you could not have lit up my understanding no better right then, of how some skunks get that way. Many of the criminal types I've had cause to arrest, have been from terrible backgrounds where they was taught nothin' but meanness, unkindness and badness — none of it their fault.

Still, as much as I sympathize with 'em, I'm still gonna do what I have to when dealin' with any hard cases. And there comes a point when such bad behaviors become a choice that they made, not just what they was driven to.

Killing innocent people, for instance. That's a choice only truly bad men make.

The day being halfway between cool and warm, she brought coffee and tea to the porch, and we all got caught up. Seemed Mavis had done wonders for the welfare of all the children, just as Emmett had told us. Only thing was, Mavis Benson refused to take credit for all her fine work.

She bided her time and waited til Mary went off to the outhouse, then she brought up an important matter.

"Mister and Mrs Frakes," she said then, "Just last week I received a letter from the City, and I must say, I found it quite puzzling. The truth is, I believed it must surely have been a mistake. But it turns out it wasn't. At least, the *reason* for the letter was valid, and it's very good that you're here, for it concerns Mary."

I felt a great panic rising within me, but managed to bite down my feelings so I could speak. "Some problem of paperwork," I said, "regarding the child's adoption?"

"No, not that," she answered to my great relief, before looking around to make certain the child wasn't on her way back yet. "It was a letter, addressed to myself, warning that if I do not pay the rates that are owed on a property I own, the place will be sold to anyone who pays the tariff. It falls due two weeks from now."

Georgina looked at her sideways, like one a'them flummoxed dogs you see sometimes, when they can't quite make sense of a thing.

But me, I'm more used to the workings of Law than my wife is — and used to the way skunks turn things to their own advantage, whether it's wrong or wronger.

"The property belonged to Mary's folks," I suggested, and Mavis agreed, "Yes it did."

"Your husband came by it somehow, and put it into your name, but he never told you."

"Exactly that, Mister Frakes," she replied. "I looked through what I thought was old papers that didn't much matter, and found the deed in amongst them. It was dated just two days after the death of her parents. Two days after Mary came here to live. I was shocked, of course. And there are other properties too."

Mary had come out of the outhouse, but had wandered away to pick flowers that grew near the fence, so we kept our voices low enough not to be heard, and kept talking.

"A year ago," I said, "when your husband August threatened me and Deputy Slaughter, the skunk dropped heavy-handed hints about him having powerful friends — even named one such, Mayor Fisk. Was that all a bag of hot air, or was it a true enough fact, Ma'am?"

"August — *may he rot in Hell* — and that gosh-darn Mayor, Reginald Fisk, were thick as two thieves," she said, gripping her teacup so hard it's a wonder she never busted it up into pieces. "And when I went to speak to the Mayor of this yesterday, he told me not to worry about it, it was all a mistake. Said that he'd find me a buyer, though the place isn't worth much anyway."

"Strange you only got the letter just now. Rate notice shoulda been sent at the start of the year." I gulped down my coffee, as I realized it had gone almost cold, and said, "Good coffee, that."

"Arbuckles, of course, Mister Frakes. Yes, our own rate notice came as per usual, yet no notices came for the Wilson place. I never did trust the Mayor, and the whole thing seemed underhanded to me. So after I walked out of the building, I waited a few moments then sneaked back inside. And sure enough, Mayor Fisk was bawling out a young man who was new to his job. Threatened to end his employment if he sent out such notices again before consulting Fisk personally."

"Filthy dang skunk," I growled, smacking my right fist into the palm of my other hand so hard it hurt — *should maybe not have hit that giant QUITE so hard with my old hands*. I winced a little and added, "So what *do* we do, Missus Benson?"

"First thing we do, is you both start calling me *Mavis*. Less reminders of my former husband the better, I think."

"Fair enough too, Mavis," I replied with a nod of agreement.

"And secondly, we do the right thing by Mary, if it's alright with you. That place *is* hers, so it should go into your name, I believe, at least until she's of age. I've made enquiries elsewhere, and it's worth a lot more than our corrupt little Mayor would have had me believe. I've not paid the rates yet, but I'd be happy to pay them as a token of—"

"You're a good woman, Mavis," I said, and Georgina heartily agreed. "I'll pay what's owing, a'course, you've done so much for Mary already. Perhaps we could meet up in town one day this week, get the deed transferred and notarized proper. But here comes Mary now, I guess we should see how she feels about it, before we do anything else."

As Mary came bounding toward us, she wore a big happy smile, her hands hidden behind her back until she arrived.

Then, with a laugh and a flourish, she whipped her hands round in front of her, and presented a small bunch of flowers to each of the women, before saying, "My first mother grew these at our lovely home, and I'm sure she'd approve of me gifting them to the two special ladies who carried on her work raising me. Thank you both."

"Oh, Mary," both women said together, accepting the flowers she offered. "Thank you."

"I know what we could do, perhaps later this week," Mary said brightly then. "Perhaps we could take a nice ride out to see my old home. I've never been there, you know, since my parents were killed there. And while it would be tinged with sadness, the happy memories I have of the place would surely outweigh my melancholy. *Can* we go, Father? Can we?"

"Tinged?" I said, shaking my head like as if that might clear it. *"Melon-WHATTY?* And you reckon *I'm* the one talks funny. Well a'course we can go have a look. But button your mouth now and open your ears, Mary Frakes. Seems like Mavis has good news to tell you."

CHAPTER 15
BLACK-TAILED DEER

Mavis Benson had other appointments in town, so we arranged to meet her at City Hall, over on Seventeenth Street, at two o'clock.

Mary had cried tears of joy when she heard that she was to have the Wilson place returned to her for her own, just as it should be.

On the ride back to town, we warned her that the place would be in poor condition, after having sat there unused for two years.

"Might be a family a'bears moved into the place yet," I told her.

Undaunted, she countered with, "That would be surprising and *wonderful!* Most *especially* if they like porridge!"

That child sure is a delight, and a gift every day a'my life.

We had some hours to kill, and as me and Emmett had

decided to not make no noises round town til we went back to see Delvene Abbott again, I had not much to do, and noplace to do it.

So me and my girls decided on a big slap-up meal, at our favorite restaurant. I chose the black-tailed deer, and got 'em to heap up my plate with so many tasty vegetables it took me ten minutes of chomping til I found the meat.

Sure was worth it though — ever you get the chance, make sure to try black-tailed deer. Not sure what makes it so tasty compared to them with lighter tails, but I promise it is so.

Mary tried to tell me that true black-tailed deer are only found near the coast, but I told her that's because the ones near the coast is all slower, on account of the relaxing sea air.

"Fact is," I said, "we're lucky anyone finds 'em at all, they's so good at hiding away. So maybe we should all eat up and stop gabbing about it."

She just stuck her tongue out at me — but I didn't say nothin' about it, as I like it when she acts her true age. *Children SHOULD play up some, it's good for their spirit.* So I stuck *my* tongue out too, then we both looked at Georgina, to make sure we hadn't got caught.

I *had* planned to have a beer with my meal, but Georgina pulled rank, telling me I should retain a clear head for when we went to get the deed to Mary's property put in our name.

Well, I ain't sure who made Georgina the General in this family, but I do know how to take orders — I didn't argue the point, and enjoyed a nice sarsaparilla with my meal instead.

Not sure *why* my good wife thinks one beer can ruin a man's normal docity[1] — might be she seen it writ up on some Temperance sign someplace or another.

Sarsaparilla goes better with black-tailed deer anyway — and also, beer sits too heavy when you've eaten too much, way I did today.

Right on two, we met up with Mavis, and we had a quick discussion about how things might go. Mavis was certain Mayor Fisk would get himself involved, and probably try to change her mind about things.

"It seemed *very* important to him somehow," she said. "Though he tried to make out it was nothing at all. But I've known the man a good while, he has *some* sort of trick up his sleeve."

"Suits me fine if he gets involved," I said. "I ain't never met the man, and I'd like the chance to take my *own* measure of him."

"He'll measure short on decency," said Mavis, "and long on sneakiness. But watch him, Lyle, don't underestimate the man, he's a *very* clever fellow indeed."

I nodded slowly, looked to my wife and child, seen they was paying close attention. "We'll all keep our eyes and ears open in that case — and you women can keep your brains working on it as well. Me lacking in brains, I'll just do the talking — which a'course, I'll only do *if* he won't listen to you, Mavis, or gives you trouble."

"So Fisk won't know who *you* are by sight?" Mavis asked me.

"Don't reckon so," I replied. "I ain't never met him before. Any chance he might recognize Mary?"

"He never once came to the Orphanage, not even when August was alive. He'll have no idea who *any* of you are until he sees your name on the paperwork when we all sign it."

"Good," I said. "Folks are less careful when they don't yet know I'm an ex-lawman. He might let something slip if he thinks he's just dealing with an ordinary bearded old coot. Let's go on in."

"A quiet word first, Lyle, please." Mavis said, and we two stepped away from my girls a few moments.

"Must be good if you can't say it in front a'my family."

"I would *never* speak of such things in front of a child," she whispered. "And it's *probably* not even relevant — but I know for an absolute *truth* that Mayor Fisk has been spending time with Sheriff Cal Pettygore's wife, while the Sheriff is working. Half the town knows, it seems. She likes the Mayor for his cleverness — do you *know* the Sheriff yourself?"

"Not the sharpest arrow in the quiver, Cal Pettygore," I said.

"Well, that's why Maude Pettygore went looking elsewhere — at least that's what she told a mutual friend. I just thought I'd let *you* know, Lyle. They're supposedly good friends, you see, the Mayor and the Sheriff. But the friendship goes only one way. That's the sort of man Reginald Fisk *really* is."

"Duly noted," I said, slowly shaking my head.

Somethin' wrong with some fellers.

I held the door open for the ladies — Mavis went first, then Mary and Georgina. I followed behind as we walked down the wide entry corridor of City Hall — nothin' in here but two big fancy paintings — then we entered the room where they conduct public business.

The young feller at the counter seemed mightily flustered when Mavis told him what was happening. He excused himself for a minute, claiming he'd run out of ink and had to go fetch some from the supply room.

Mavis smiled knowingly at him, then when he was gone she said, "That's the young man who got bawled out by the Mayor last time I was here. And that door he went through leads to Mayor Fisk's private office, *not* the supply room."

We soon heard the poor young feller gettin' yelled at again, something about him having interrupted a meeting of utmost importance, followed by, "What? Why didn't you let me know sooner, you inconsequential excuse for a man!"

But we had our own entertainments, right here where we were.

"Look," Mary said with a laugh. "He has a whole *bottle* of ink here unopened, besides what he has in his inkwell."

I picked up the spare bottle, checked that the lid was on tight, and dropped it in my coat pocket.

"*Lyle Frakes!*" Georgina exclaimed. "Put that ink back this minute."

But I only laughed and said, "What ink? You heard the young feller, he ain't got no ink. I can't steal what never existed, now can I? *Well, can I?*"

1. DOCITY: Comprehension, clear understanding.

CHAPTER 16
ALL BLUSTER AND BULLDUST

Mavis sure seen the funny side when I pilfered the young feller's ink. She barely managed to compose herself as the Mayor strode into the room, full of his own self-importance.

He weren't short exactly, but somehow he *seemed* that way to me. All bluster and bulldust he was, as he walked in spouting insincere words of greeting at Mavis Benson.

"Mavis, my *dear woman,*" he was saying. But he stopped in his tracks when he cast a glance in my direction, stood adjusting his necktie and looked from me back to Mavis. "Please, Mavis, step through to my office. Your friends may wait for you here, as we have private business to conduct."

"That's fine, Reginald," she said, a hint of a smile playing at her lips. "My business can be done with the clerk today. You can get back to your own important business, I know your job is a busy one."

The officious little skunk's eyes darted from each of our

faces to the next — except for Georgina's, she had hid herself back behind us, way she often does — then he looked right at Mavis, chose his words careful-like.

"There seems to have been a misunderstanding, my dear woman. My clerk tells me you wish to sell the old Wilson property to a buyer you've brought along with you. But as per your recent instructions, I've already sold the place for a very fair price." Then turning to me he added, "A pity you've wasted your time, sir, but you'll have to find another property, I'm afraid. Such go the tides of fortune, these modern times."

Well, Mavis Benson might not have been in the driver's seat long, but she sure weren't no fool when it come to business.

"Reginald Fisk," she began. "I've known you a good many years, and I must say, I never did like you."

"Now, Mavis, you surely don't mean—"

"Oh, I think I know what I mean, Reg."

"I prefer to be called—"

"Yes, Reg, I know you do," she said, her smile cold as her eyes bored holes through the man. "But I truly don't care *what* you prefer. And if you're telling the truth, Reg — that you have indeed sold *my* property without my knowledge or signature, well, I think I'll just run along and report that to the Law. Because last time I checked, it was illegal to sell a place you don't own."

"Mavis, please, not in front of these strangers, I'm sure we can—"

"Well, Reg, which is it? Did you break the *law?* Or did you *lie* to me just now? It's one or the other. Which one?"

Two minutes ago he had strutted into the room like a fine bantam rooster, all full of himself and prepared to run over the top of us all, to take whatever he wanted. But now he looked like she had wrung his fool neck, and he seemed about ready to be plucked and dropped into the stew.

He took a deep breath, tried to pull himself together and said in a dignified sorta voice, "Mavis, tell me. How much *is* the man's offer? It's my strong opinion I can get my *own* man to do better."

"Ain't none a'your business," I growled. "You best scurry on back to your office, lest I lose my temper and throw you outta that window into the street."

"How *dare* you, sir. I am the Mayor of Cheyenne. I will *not* be threatened by a mere ruffian." He cast an eye over my buckskins, huffed some and added, "I don't know how you *people* do things in the mountains, but here in the cities we are decent and civilized. We have no need of violent threats, in order to do business. Now answer me. How *much* is the offer?"

I smiled the sorta smile any clever man would have understood as a warning to shut the hell up. "Fisk," I said. "The offer is this — you slink back to your office and stop wasting our time, and I'll let you go, still in one piece. I reckon that's more than fair."

"It's more than he usually offers," said Mary.

"Quite generous I thought," said Georgina.

"Goodbye, Reg," said Mavis.

"Five-hundred," he said, eyes wide open as he backed away to the door he came in by. "That's more than it's worth, Mavis, *please*. You've put me in an awkward position, I've already accepted the man's money."

"How about two-thousand dollars?" Mary said, which surprised every one of us — most especially Fisk. "As we've already paid seven-hundred, we could make a quick profit. I believe that might work out for both parties."

You coulda knocked me down with a barn swallow's tail-feather, and Georgina and Mavis had to look the other way to hide their smiles.

"Why, it's not worth *nearly* that much, little girl," he said, turning his attention on her, but still ready to flee if he had to.

"Well, I hear it's quite a *nice* place," Mary said.

A half-smile came to his face, but he hid it quick. "Its *true* value is only three-hundred, you see, unimproved as it is. But the nice man who wishes to buy it has *other* holdings nearby, and wishes to consolidate, you see. Therefore, I could perhaps speak with him, get him to go to ... a thousand?" Then he turned to address me and said, "Have you actually *seen* the property, sir?"

He was a well practiced liar, but there was *something* not quite straight in how he had said it.

"Never seen it," I told him. "But Mavis here said it ain't much, what she's heard."

He smiled like a cat who found out the bird-cage door is busted and about to fall open. "Terrible place, sir, I've seen it. You should take the thousand and put it toward something better."

"No. I don't think so," Mary said then. "Please send in

the clerk, I've changed my mind. We're quite attached to the idea of *this* place, you see."

"It's simply business is all, little girl," the skunk said. "No sense getting sentimental about it, that won't do at all."

It was Mary's turn now to bore holes in that skunk with her eyes, and her words came out hard at the edges, but she did not cry. "I grew up on that place, Mister Mayor. My parents were *killed* there. And if you think I'm being *sentimental,* you can eat a boot-full of dung, you awful, horrible, *nasty* excuse for a man."

An expression of horror came over him, as he realized just who we were. Then his terrified gaze went to me — and he fled without saying a word.

Me, I only said three.

The first one was *Stinkin'*.

The second was *Damn*.

And the third word, you know it was *Skunk*.

CHAPTER 17
FAST HORSES

"The look on the pathetic man's face!" Georgina laughed, as we all climbed into our beds later that night.

I reckon it was the tenth time she'd said it, but even so, the memory of it remained a strong source of amusement.

"I do believe, Father," said Mary, "that he thought you might *actually* throw him out of the window. I've never seen anyone disappear quite so quickly."

"He's lucky he did," I said. "Makin' me cuss in front of three ladies that way. Might go back for a visit tomorrow, take him up on the roof and see if he can fly."

"You'll do nothing of the sort," said Georgina, shutting down the last of the lights so we were in darkness. "The paperwork's done, and we have no further business with the horrid fellow. And besides, he'd have the Sheriff arrest you, I'm certain — and *then* how will we ever find Jesse Gillespie?"

We went off to sleep then, and I dreamed of horses and

pastures and hammers, and bathtubs too for some reason. Some folks claim our dreams mean a whole lotta somethin' important, but I reckon maybe our minds lose control of our senses when we go off to sleep, and it ain't worth givin' our dreams one moment of thought once we's lucid again.

Nice word that — lucid, I mean — Mary taught me it one day when we discussed dreaming, a little over a year ago not far from here. Reckon we should maybe go on a trip soon, visit old friends. Sure can't beat a crackling campfire out on the trail, for a fine place to talk about life and its unknown meanings.

We woke good and early, and at first Mary grumbled when I shook her and said to get up.

"Alright, suits me," I told her. "I don't care about watchin' fast horses run round in a circle. I'll go back to bed, you can wake me at noon with a plateful of bacon."

"Trackwork," she cried, and she leaped outta bed with such speed poor Princess Mussbeetle flew across the room and landed under the dresser. "Sorry, my dear Princess Mayblossom," called Mary, and she giggled a little and retrieved the sorely aggrieved pile a'rags, before kissing it on both button eyes and placing it back on the pillow.

An hour later we were out at the track, and so was half the dang townsfolk, you shoulda seen 'em. Even at that hour some a'them fancier fellers was wearing their suits, had their hair all slicked back with grease, and smelled like they'd been spending time in a dirt cheap bordello.

Come to think of it, maybe they had. Lazy rich folk ain't always the best at wakin' up early, so maybe that'd be a good strategy for a sort of alarm clock. Better than a real one anyway, all a'that whizzin' and ringin' they do — scares the life from a man, such a clock does.

Not that I'd know what it's like to wake in a bordello. Just somethin' I heard about from a friend, that's all I'm sayin' about it, so don't get accusatory at me.

Soon as there was enough light for horses to run by, they all started a'running. Sometimes fast, sometimes slow — sometimes alone, or cantering in pairs, before rushing the last two furlongs to the finish at a gallop.

Well, Mary *said* it was two furlongs – looked like about a quarter-mile to me, but what would I know about racing?

I kept both ears open, and pointed my eyes every which way, for any old thing that might help us. I might not know much about horse-racing, but I do know this — when folks get their attention all focused on one thing, they stop paying attention to others. And sometimes, then, they let secrets slip outta their mouths.

And that's what I was listening for.

Me and Emmett had decided to keep mostly apart for two reasons — first thing, we didn't want anyone cottoning on that we was investigating the murders. And as long as Delvene Abbott didn't give up the game, Sheriff Cal Pettygore weren't nohow likely to suspect we was doing so.

The other reason me and Emmett kept apart was a simple and logical one — by being in two separate places, we was two times as likely to hear something useful, a'course. More than that really, as even the most foolish of men will stay on their guard when a lawman's around. But there's plenty of folks who don't know me by sight, and see me as some doddering fool who's likely half-deaf and three-quarters drunk.

I split up from my family too — kept an eye out for 'em, a'course, but I hung back a ways, and Georgina too kept her ears open. She and Mary watched the horses from down by the rail — the child sure was excited when the animals come thundering past just a few feet away.

Thing was, I never heard anything useful while the horses were running. All the talk then was of speeds and stamina and times the sharps[1] read off their watches, then noted down next to names they all seemed to know.

Toward the end of the gallops, Emmett Slaughter walked past, slightly bumping me and making a signal no one else woulda noticed. I looked where he'd directed me to, and seen right away who it was — the Abbott boys, without doubt, both riding horses to the watering bays, their gallops having finished.

One Abbott looked like his father, and the other looked like his mother — before she growed so large, anyway.

Fine horses they were on too — their coats all a'gleam in the early morning sun, their hot breath blowing great clouds of steam into the still air as they pranced in that athletic way only thoroughbreds do.

Quite something, that pair a'horses, even I could see that. I bet they could gallop up a storm. Might even have a bet raceday myself, just on the looks a'that pair.

I made my way across to stand near the watering bays — not too close, but where I could hear from. But I weren't the only one. Now all the gallops was finished, it seemed every man and his dog wished to congregate there, so I just blended in, watched and listened.

And to my surprise — well, I might shoulda almost suspected — I seen a face most familiar.

And I smiled to myself, for he was not only a friend I was happy to see, but also a man who knew more about horses and racing then any man I ever knew.

I would wait til the crowd was thinned out, and remake his acquaintance.

---

1. SHARP: Someone who IS sharp, clever and capable. A Racetrack Sharp is a clever feller, in the same way a Card Sharp is — and he might even be honest too. Well, maybe...

CHAPTER 18
SNEAKIN' ABOUT

As I watched the proceedings, it was clear my old friend was in high demand. Seemed like he had more friends than a top painted dove in a mining town — one who's decided to make her services free for the day.

My friend was respected for his knowledge, no doubt — but also, folks *do* love a winner. And from all the talk that I heard nearby, it seemed that his horse had won the Cup Race in Sidney four days ago — and was a hot favorite to repeat its success in Cheyenne, just three days from now.

He was trying his best to attend to his horses — he and his stable-boy, I mean — but some of the rich types in suits seemed to think my old friend had nothing better to do than to answer their questions.

No one paid much attention to the Abbotts, but as I watched them walk their horses away, I saw my good wife and child *'accidentally'* cross their path, and as Mary stroked the necks of their horses, Georgina engaged the men in conversation.

It was clever to do so, a'course — though I could not help but be worried. Thing was, for all we knew these *could* be the men who had killed Mary's parents — the things Red said *may* have been true, but then, they also may not.

Dying men tend to scramble their words when the pain's bad, even though they're compelled toward truth — and Red's pain must have been terrible, gutshot as he was, and so close to his death when Emmett found him.

And too, Red MIGHT have been protecting his brothers, his words all being lies to throw Emmett off of the scent.

What we needed was more information, some solid place to get started.

But now I thought more about that, I realized *Emmett* must have pointed the Abbott boys out to Georgina — and that he would also be watching from some hidden vantage point. And without any doubt, my wife was the *perfect* person to find out what they knew, without raising any suspicions.

She just has a certain *way* about her that gets folks to offer up all their truth — more truth than they *meant* to tell.

How do I know that? Well, if YOU are married to a clever woman — and let's face it, there ain't no other sort — I reckon you can guess for yourself how I know, from experience.

The Mayor too was here watching proceedings, standing beside the damn Sheriff — *skunks sure do love each other's company* — and when that pair seen me they put their heads together, then spoke fast and furtive, as if of some terrible secret.

Their heads darted this way and that like two prairie dogs suddenly afeared of somethin' seen at a distance.

I gave 'em a nod and a smile a'course, just to put some wind under their tails. Even took off my hat and waved it right at 'em, in case it weren't clear I had seen 'em there plotting together. They didn't like *that* much — but it ain't my job to be liked.

Sooner Cheyenne is rid of 'em both, the better this place will be.

Seeing as how Sheriff Cal Pettygore was watching me, I didn't go near Georgina and Mary. I don't like Cal, but he ain't a *complete* fool. And him being in tandem with the Mayor, well, I'd have to be careful.

And I'm certain Mavis Benson was right — that little skunk Mayor was a clever one.

I'd have *liked* to have spoke to the Abbotts myself, but if the Mayor found out I'd done so, he'd be certain I knew *something*. And besides, them brothers would likely know who I was.

Also, if the Sheriff *really* killed Red — and certainly, the Mayor was *somehow* mixed up in acquiring the Wilson place for *someone* — might be that they was involved in the deaths of the Wilsons back then.

The Wilsons were killed for *some* reason. And so far, the only possible reason we'd found amounted to the value of their little property. And the Mayor seemed quite keen to have it for someone he knew.

Then again, a hundred-sixty acres with a small log

cabin ain't worth *nearly* enough for most men to kill for — especially not men like the Mayor and the Sheriff, who were somewhat well-off, and had enough power to make money without killing for it.

No, that ain't it, Lyle. Stop thinking and get watching again.

At least from where the Mayor and Sheriff now stood, they could not see the Abbotts, like I could. The Mayor would recognize Mary from the previous day, and I didn't want that.

What I needed was to get Mary away, just in case the Mayor wandered in that direction. Lucky for me, young Roy Grimm came limping by then with a horse he had just helped a feller rub down, so I said, "Hey there, Roy, could you let Mary know to meet me where our horses are waiting, quick as she can? Let her know it's important, and to go right away."

"Just Mary, Mister Frakes, not your missus?"

"That's right, Roy. I'll see you in a few hours. We'll be back late afternoon."

A half-minute later, Mary looked over at me, then turned and smiled at Roy. She gave the Abbott horses one final rub on their necks, and walked off to where our horses was waiting.

I went there by a different route, disappearing into the crowd, and we collected our animals and moved them into some shade, as the morning was starting to get over-warm for the season.

"Those men are the Abbotts," Mary told me.

"I know they are, child. Did you and your Mother tell them your names while you spoke?"

"No, Father, I don't think it was that sort of talk. People here are more focused on *horses* than regular niceties — in a way, I really quite like it."

"What *was* said then, Mary? Just the headlines, not the whole story."

"Well, let's see," she said, scratching her chin the way an old man on a porch might, as he summons some almost-lost memory back to his mind. "Mother told them she has a high opinion of their horses, but they said those two always finish last. She knows more about horses than she lets on, I think. Don't you think so too, Father?"

"She knows more about *people* too," I said with a nod of agreement. "I still got a few folks to eavesdrop on, Mary. I just didn't want the Mayor to see *you* near the Abbotts."

"But wouldn't he see Mother anyway?"

"She never said much yesterday, and he paid her no mind. You and me done all the speaking, would be my main meaning — he'll remember us two for certain. And besides, that bonnet she's got on today hides her face for the most part. You wait here with the horses while I finish up, and we'll all meet back here pretty soon."

I wandered back to see that the crowd had thinned out some, and my old friend was finally getting some peace. He looked up and seen me, and a look of fond recognition came over his features — no doubt, I wore that look too.

He turned and spoke to his stable-boy a moment, then began to walk in my direction. But when he was still twenty yards off, I pointed him toward Mary.

He stopped in his tracks, looked where I'd pointed, and seemed flummoxed a moment or two. But then he noticed what I'd meant him to see, and instead of coming to me, he walked over to Mary and our horses.

She was about to get quite a surprise.

CHAPTER 19

"THE GREATEST HORSEMAN WHO EVER TOUCHED A SADDLE-BLANKET..."

By this time the Abbotts had left, and Georgina walked up beside me and started to speak. Not wanting her to miss the fun, I placed a finger against her lips, pointed then toward Mary and said, "Watch and listen, Princess, this'll be quite worth seeing."

We moved closer and watched Mary look up at my friend, and we heard him say, "That's some real fine horseflesh you got yourself there, Miss. Don't suppose you might sell me the pony?"

Georgina went to say something, but I hushed her and said, "Just watch and listen, it's fine."

Mary only smiled at the man and politely replied, "Well of *course* I could *never* entertain such an offer, but I *am* very happy to know you're a good judge of horses, sir. This pony is Dewdrop, and ... well, dear oh dear, she certainly seems to like *you!* But I *never* could sell her, she's the finest, most wonderful pony between here and

Montana — or maybe even Australia, or *anywhere* else — why, she's the best that there is."

"That a fact?" he said, as little Dewdrop rubbed her face against his and he laughed. "Well, I see she's a *real* affectionate type, but she seems to me poorly trained. I'll give you a hundred, and that's a good offer, you won't do no better'n that."

"Oh no," Mary said, quite indignant. "Why, my wonderful Dewdrop would be worth many *thousands,* not that it matters, for love's more important than money *any* old day. And as to her being poorly trained, you could not be more wrong if you said she was a giraffe."

"Looks bad trained to me," he said, rubbing Dewdrop's ears, and using his free hand to pat Horse's face, for he too was after attention from an old friend.

"Indeed, sir," Mary said. "I'll have you know that the man who trained this fine pony was the *greatest* horseman who ever touched a saddle-blanket. I don't suppose the name Wally *Davis* means anything to you?"

She stood, hands on hips now, defiantly challenging him, and he surely did rise to that challenge.

"Wally *Davis,"* he said, like as if them two words described something you'd scrape off your boot. "Not much of a horseman at all, Wally Davis. Don't know nothin' of horses, he don't, and can't ride one to save his own life."

"How dare you," she cried. "Get away from my horses, you mean nasty man!"

But he weren't finished yet by a long shot, and with a glint in his eye he went on. "Why, now I think on it, I've seen horses ride *other* horses, with a whole lot more style than ol' Wally Davis himself *ever* rode. No, someone's been tellin' you tall ones, I reckon, young miss. It's no wonder your pony's so poorly behaved. But thanks for lettin' me know Wally trained her — I sure won't be buyin' her now."

Well the look that crossed poor Mary's face was one you coulda sold to the army if it coulda been bottled.

And I couldn't take it no more, I busted out laughing.

As Mary heard my laugh and spun round to face me, her look went from rage to bewilderment, and I said, "Congratulations, Mary, you just met the finest horseman this side of Australia. Wally Davis, meet my daughter Mary. You know Horse and Dewdrop already, and this here beside me's Georgina, my long-suffering wife."

He busted out laughing too, and little Mary's look changed again — this time from bewilderment to awe; then it changed once again into something like adoration.

"Wally Davis," she cried. "It's really you, Wally Davis, who trained Dewdrop and left her with dear Mister Silver, so he could give her to whichever child would need her! Oh, no *wonder* my dear Dewdrop loved you so much when she saw you. Why of *course* you're Wally Davis! Goodness me, I *should* have known."

CHAPTER 20
COLD HARD TRUTHS

We didn't have time to catch up much, on account of Wally havin' the welfare of his horses to attend to.

Turned out he was staying at a Livery just outside the main part of town, owned and run by a feller called Godfrey Stilson. I had never met Stilson, but he had a reputation for adequate horse care, fair prices, and clean well-run premises too.

From what I understood, he was a solid enough feller, but not a horseman of highest quality, way Wally was — *or* young Roy Grimm, for that matter.

Roy was ruined for riding, with that bad leg a'his. But he understood horses like as if he was one himself. He sure could look after 'em well – good as Wally could, maybe.

I arranged to meet up with Wally for dinner that evening. He told me he trusted his stable-boy to keep watch on the horses, and said too, that he would *need* to.

"Problem with having good horses, there's always some

snake out to get 'em. And one a'mine's the Cup favorite, so we gotta watch her every minute, night and day, lest someone gets at her."

"That means someone might try to drug or injure her, Father," said Mary.

I nodded and thanked her for explaining, as if I would not have knowed what it meant without her help.

Oh, I knew it alright, and only too well. As a former lawman, I've seen things done to horses that men shoulda got their necks stretched for. But I didn't let that on to Mary. Let her keep her innocence for now, is my policy when I can manage it. She'll learn all sorts a'cold hard truths before long.

But a'course, she's learned one a'the worst ones already, when her parents was murdered two years back.

She's mostly so cheerful and happy, I sometimes forget what she's been through.

When me and Georgina and Mary mounted up for our ride back to town, I asked the child how she thought she'd go if we three raced each other round the track.

"Why, I'd *certainly* win," she announced with her wonderful laugh. "You and Mother are *much* too old to run so very far, I'd win by a mile!"

I tried not to laugh, and looked across at Georgina.

"Mary," she said, clearly close to laughing herself. "I believe your father *meant* that we might have a *horse* race."

"Oh," the child said. "Oh, of course. It *is* a racetrack for horses after all, isn't it? Well, I do believe I *would* still win."

I looked down at her short-legged pony, then at the gray Georgina rode, then back to Mary. "I reckon you're wrong about that, you young scamp. Horse here might be old, but he's a lot sounder these days since he breathed all that good ocean air for a year. And that young gray a'your mother's, he's got some speed when a good rider urges him on, and that's who's on him right now. You may not know this, but the Silver Princess there's as good a horsewoman as ever cinched up a saddle."

"Well," Mary said, "we'll just have to test it. But not *today,* of course, for you promised we could go have a look at our Wilson-Frakes family property, and I'm *rather* eager to see it."

We went along a side-trail I knew, so we didn't have to go back through town. I had a uneasy feeling in my bones, and didn't want nobody knowing where we was headed.

Mary's old place was just a couple of miles from the Abbott Ranch, so I figured we might go see Delvene while we was out there.

Seeing the racehorses run had stirred all of us up, is my best guess — not just us two-legged critters, but our horses as well — and when we came to a nice wide bit of trail with no real potholes to speak of, we all sorta looked at each other as we thought the same thing.

"Reckon it's three-hundred yards to that giant cottonwood," I announced. "Last one there has to gather all the wood for the fire and cook lunch!"

Well a'course, I'd took too long in sayin' it, and me and Horse was left standing as the others took off hell-for-leather.

Dewdrop was quick off the mark — part quarter-horse,

I wouldn't reckon — but them little legs a'hers sorely limited her top speed.

Georgina coulda gone right on by before long, but she was just relishing the feeling of being on a horse again. So instead of going past Dewdrop and Mary, she put all her energy into running a block against me and Horse.

Horse was quick though, and clever too — feigned to go right but went left, and we got up beside them a moment. But danged if Georgina didn't take her left foot from the stirrup and kick it toward us, and steer that way too.

"Hey, watch it," I called as Horse shied away some. And by then, Dewdrop and Mary had the race in their keeping.

"Won in a canter," was how the child explained it when we all stopped just past the big cottonwood. "Dewdrop first, easing down, by ten lengths, from Swayback Lightning second, with Pale-Eye Champion Blaze at the rear, after tardiness at the jump. The winner landing a betting plunge, paying odds of fifteen to one!"

"Pity you never got a bet on," I said.

"Oh, there was a bet, Lyle Frakes," said Georgina, smiling. "Make sure to grab plenty of firewood while we have a rest — and don't burn the steaks I brought with me, they're too good to waste."

CHAPTER 21
A NASTY SURPRISE AT THE WILSON PLACE

W e got a mighty surprise when we got to the Wilson place — and it didn't have nothin' to do with there being no firewood.

Indeed, when we came to the place, we seen there was plenty of wood cut to last quite a while — it was all stacked up on the porch of the house, and smoke was painting a trail from chimney to sky.

Mary looked at it in disbelief. "There's somebody living in my home."

I rested a hand on her shoulder as we all sat our horses and looked at the place from two-hundred yards off. "You're certain this is the one, child?"

"Yes, this is it. But that second barn wasn't there — we only had one."

"Couldn't be a mistake, you not having been here two years?"

"No, Father," she said. "I'm certain. Look there, where the drive goes in off the trail. My daddy put those posts in himself, and my mommy held the ladder steady while he nailed the rail onto the top of them. If we ride down there now, you'll see the name Wilson carved into the post on the left. And look how pretty the creek is, the curve of it where it runs through. And how daddy so cleverly dug a trench to go under the outhouse and carry away the ... well, you know. So he didn't have to bury it."

Georgina gripped my forearm tightly. "What do we do, Kit? We can't very well ride on in, just in case whoever is in there thinks we have no rights. Perhaps the Mayor rented it to them, and that's why he—"

"I had about enough a'that dang banty rooster, the *Mayor*. It don't matter to me *what* the occupant thinks — or what he *don't* think, for that matter. This place is Mary's, and no one has rights to be here without her permission. I'm ridin' on in to remove 'em."

"You will *stop* right this second," Georgina told me.

But she might's well have told me to invent a flying machine and go sit on some clouds. I had my dander up, and I didn't feel like waiting, discussing, or thinking.

It was time now for *doing*.

"You get back here, Lyle Frakes," came her voice from back where I'd left her.

"You two wait right there," I called over my shoulder. "I expected *some* sort of animals to be in the place, after two years deserted. Just turned out they was skunks that moved in, I'm willing to wager."

"Lyle Frakes," she called. "They might be perfectly innocent people. Don't you *hurt* anybody! Oh, Lyle, stop, we're coming with you!"

She refused to take no for an answer, and Mary, as usual, took Georgina's side. But it didn't much matter, way it went.

When we got to the gateway, Mary pointed out where it said *Wilson,* and ran her hand over the carving. She didn't cry, not exactly — but the tears were right there at the edge of her, like you'd expect of a ten-year-old, that situation.

Thing was, there weren't no actual gate anyway. Just them three logs, put in place by honest owners, proclaiming their pride in their home.

But since they'd been murdered here, some other rotten damn skunk had been making use of the land as well as the home. Place had been grazed within an inch of its life at some point — there was patches of nothin' but weeds told the tale — but most of it was recovered by now. And there was an almost-new good-sized corral, with a half-dozen horses inside it.

Ordinary horses that cowhands would ride, not thoroughbreds, was the next thought I had.

I woulda preferred my two girls to let me go alone, but they had their danders up too. And it is Mary's property, after all.

We rode in together, and I had Gertrude ready, just in case there was any unfriendliness coming our way.

"Hail the house," I called when we got to within fifty yards.

We halted and waited there several moments, and it seemed maybe no one was there. Then the door of the place swung open, and a long lean cowhand stumbled out onto the porch. He was dressed only in his unmentionables, no boots or hat, but he carried a thumping great pistol — biggest six-shooter I ever saw, and he looked in no proper condition to hold up the weight of it.

He squinted some and said, "That ain't you is it, Boss? I weren't feelin' well, but I'll—"

"I ain't your boss, son," I called. "And where's your dang *clothes*? Get inside and get decent then come on back out."

"Who the hell are *you*, mister?" he cried. "Get off a'this private land or I'll fill you so full of holes, there'll be piss comin' outta your ... hey, them others with you is women and children." Well his tone sure changed then, went respectful. "I'm sorry, Ma'am — and you too Miss — I never meant to scare you or cuss in your presence, that was rude of me and I apologize. Could you tell me why you're all here?"

Before I could answer, Georgina said, "Let *me* speak to him, Kit, you have a way of fanning sparks into wildfires, and I don't think we need that right now."

"Mother's right," Mary said with a smile. "You *do* upset folks needlessly sometimes. But don't worry, we still like you *most* of the time."

I could not truthfully argue, so it was Georgina who spoke to the clearly intoxicated young feller.

"Have you *rented* this house?" she called to him. "And if so, from whom?"

"*Whom?*" he went, sounding like a dang owl. "I ain't sure what that is, Ma'am."

"It just means *who.*"

"Well why didn't you say that the first time? With all due respect, I mean, Ma'am." He swayed some as he stood on the porch, before steadying himself against the post at the top of the stairs by crooking an arm round it. "I work for Orville Lannigan, Ma'am, and he allows us cowhands to use this place for a bunkhouse. This is *his* property. Guess I drank too much last night, I best swaller a big pot a'coffee and go do some work 'fore the boss hears about it. He don't tolerate such behavior, and fair enough too."

"Lannigan," I growled. "That damn snot-nosed suit-wearin' skunk. I'll tear him in forty-six bits, and shove my boot so far up his—"

"Language, Kit!" Georgina scolded. "Not in front of the child. Now *whoever* is this Lannigan fellow?"

"No one important," I told her. "Just a half-gallon head in a ten-gallon hat, who hides behind others, causin' innocent folks to lose buttons off a'their buckskins."

"We'll discuss all *that* later," said Georgina. Then to the man she called out, "Your boss has no rights of ownership here. *We* are the legal owners, and he never had any right to trespass or make use of the place. Please take a message to him informing him of it. You have until midday tomorrow to vacate the premises, at which time we will be here to move in. Do you understand the message, or shall I write it down for you to take to him?"

The feller had ceased to wave the gun around, and, suddenly noticing the state of his undress, he hightailed it round behind the post, so his trapdoors [1]was at least partly hidden. Then he looked round the edge a'the post and said,

"Vacate means to get everything out, right? Includin' our selfs and our horses?"

"That's more-or-less my understanding of the word," Georgina told him. "Well done."

"Aw, Ma-am, please. Mister Lannigan ain't gonna like that, not even a bit. Can't you go tell him yourself? It's just two miles yonder to the ranch-house."

"Best you do it," she told him. "My husband seems not to like him, so let's keep them apart, hmmm?"

"Aw, Ma'am. The boss'll sick Little Wayne Logan on me I reckon, just for bringin' the news. He's a ill-tempered feller, Mister Lannigan is, whenever he don't get his way."

"Wouldn't worry too much about Logan for awhile," I growled at the unfortunate cowhand. "Last I seen the big lump, he was havin' a sleep on the floor of Cheyenne's best saloon, with his nose spread all over his face and blood pourin' from it."

"*Little Wayne?* You sure, mister?" He then used his hands as he spoke, as if to show Logan's measurements as he described him. "Giant feller, near seven feet. And wide as two pickhandles, and muscles stacked up on his muscles?"

"The very feller," I said. "Ain't so tough as he looks, them muscles is only for show. I reckon *you'd* take him, hard-workin' cowhand like yourself, lean and rawboned as you are."

He shook his head like he thought I was loco, said, "Naw, I don't reckon to try it."

"You just take the message to Lannigan, son. And tell him from me — *it's Lyle Frakes, you got the name?* — if I see

him again, it'll be *him* I hit first, not his show-offy over-
growed muscle-man. We'll see how Lannigan fares when
he fights his own battles."

"Noon tomorrow," Georgina called. "And we'll have
lawmen with us, to make sure things stay calm and friendly.
After all, we're to be neighbors. Nice to meet you, young
man."

And we wheeled our horses about and rode off, leaving
the now sober cowhand with a flummoxed look on his face,
as he pondered his future.

———————————————

1. TRAPDOORS: Long underwear with a convenient button up flap at
the back

CHAPTER 22
THICK AS THIEVES

After leaving the Wilson place, we rode at a leisurely pace to the Abbott Ranch.

I figured Delvene Abbott's boys might be there. If that was the case, we would not go in, but keep riding past, then come out to see her tomorrow.

But as it turned out she was there all alone, putting a coat of red paint on her barn. I called to her from a distance, and she waved us on in.

"Need a hand with that painting?" I asked as we got close, and she dropped her brush in a bucket. "I got a mighty willing young worker here with me, and I reckon she'd be happy to help out for free, just to see your nice horses."

"Oh yes," Mary piped up. "I've never painted before, but it *does* look like fun, and the horses, my goodness, such magnificent thoroughbreds, every last one a fine specimen!"

"Knows her horseflesh alright," Delvene said, wiping a stray lock of hair from her face with a paint-covered hand.

Well, introduce us, Frakes, or have you forgotten your manners in your frail dotage?"

Funny thing, how I don't mind SOME people callin' me old. Ain't so bad at all when it's folks I actually like.

I nodded toward the appropriate folks as I spoke, saying, "This fearsome woman on the gray is my good wife, Georgina, and the good judge of horseflesh is our daughter, Mary. And this woman who just put red paint through her hair is my friend Delvene Abbott. I hope you don't mind being called friend, Delvene — but I reckon our previous acquaintance got us halfway, and it looks like we might soon be neighbors, if that's news you can stand."

"Well, I'm happy as a dog with two tails to be friends with your family," the big woman said with a laugh that made her wobble and bounce, one end to the other. "And you, Frakes, I can put up with. We best go inside, have some coffee and pie, in order to seal our friendship." Then she winked at Georgina and added, "Anything to get away from this painting, I been at it three hours."

It was a pleasant time we spent with her, but she hadn't found anything out that could help us.

We spoke about horses and ranches, the ocean and all sorts, and we told her of what had just happened out at the Wilson place.

At the mention of Lannigan's name her eyes hardened, but she didn't say much on that yet.

Georgina and Mary told her they'd spoke to her boys at the racetrack, and all in all it was a nice sorta talk we all had. *Just like proper neighbors should be,* was one thought I had.

I thought too, about how I've quite liked living out by the ocean, but a lotta the neighboring folks ain't exactly *my* cup of Arbuckles. Some are, a'course, most especially them few we've got to know recent. But here, round Cheyenne, I just feel like I fit in better somehow.

Anyhow, I'll think more on all that a bit later.

Georgina's talent for getting folks to share information has never diminished, and one thing we learned was why Delvene preferred to stay home.

"I always did prefer horses to people for the most part," she told us, dropping huge great dollops of fresh-whipped cream onto everyone's apple pie. "But it ain't only that. It's that rotten damn skunk you already mentioned. Orville Lannigan ain't to be trusted one bit, and I ain't one picayune[1] surprised he'd took your place over. No doubt him and the damn stinkin' mayor's thick as thieves too, you watch out for 'em both, take my warning."

Georgina grasped my arm then and said, *"That's who the buyer must have been, the one the mayor mentioned. No doubt they always planned for Lannigan to take the place over. And if the new fellow at City Hall hadn't sent out the notice to Mavis, none of us would have ever been the wiser."*

Mary showed her frustration by making two tiny fists — but it must not have been quite sufficient to disperse all her anger, for a growl soon escaped her, followed by two angry words.

"Damn thieves!"

"Mary *Frakes!*" cried Georgina. "Language!"

"Listen to your mother," I said. "We can't have you

sounding like me, folks'll think you was always a Frakes, and never a Wilson at all. You should honor the fine upbringing *they* gave you, would be my main meaning, Mary."

"Although in this *particular* case," Georgina said thoughtfully, "it was perhaps somewhat justified." And to my great surprise she too said, *"Damn thieves,"* and I struggled awhile not to laugh, but instead to take the thing serious, as was expected.

"Sorry," said Mary, her eyes shining with mirth now. "I promise I won't do it again."

As for Delvene Abbott, she could not have looked more impressed if the child had jumped a horse over her house, then turned round and done it a second time, while wearing a blindfold.

And when we finally left, she hugged the child warmly, and told her she hoped we might stay a *long* time in Cheyenne — and to visit whenever we had a spare hour or two, for we'd always be welcome.

———————————

1. PICAYUNE: Tiny. (Smaller than small, bigger than something invisible)

CHAPTER 23

ANGRIFIED!

That evening, as planned, Wally Davis met with me and my family for dinner — at the *good* restaurant, a'course.

Soon's we walked inside and took off our hats, I seen Wally had lost just about half his hair. Why, young Wally looked just about older'n'me — and I tell you, the reminder we was *both* gettin' on didn't make me feel no better.

Our food had not yet arrived when a waitress came over and asked me, "I'm sorry, sir, are you Lyle Frakes?"

"I was Frakes last time I checked."

She took out a letter from her apron pocket and handed it to me. "This was left here for you, sir. We've no idea who left it, but as you can see, it says to please give it to you when you come for dinner tonight."

"Folks sure learn a man's movements quick," I said.

"It *is* the best restaurant in town," said Georgina. "They must know how much you like your food. *Or* they saw you here just last night, that's logical, isn't it? Well, come on, what does it say?"

I unfolded it, glanced at it once, didn't like what I saw. Folded it up again before anyone else could see it. "I'll read it later. We come here to eat, not to read."

"You sound *angrified,* Father," said Mary. Then smiling at Wally she added, "That's one of Father's best and most favorite words, Mister Wally."

He threw his head backways and laughed. "A Frakes special, that word, if ever I heard one."

"Ain't *particular* angrified," I said, as I shoved the offensive piece a'paper deep in my pocket. "Just hungry is all. Just a note from a feller I met yesterday, offering me a dang job. I already told the fool no when he asked me the first time."

"Fastest I ever saw anyone read," said Georgina, raising her eyebrows in that questioning manner she sometimes employs.

I knew then she hadn't seen the letter — if she'd seen what I had, she'd have dropped it, instead of pushing things this way, with Mary right here.

Letter weren't written in pencil or ink — it was made up of bits of newsprint cut from a newspaper.

LeAve CHEYENNE oR yoUr FAmilY DiE

Ain't the sorta thing best brought up at a nice family meal. Best I examine it later.

They was all out of black-tailed deer, but it weren't too much hardship to settle for their beef rib-eye roast, all basted with lashings of butter and served up with cheesy potato mash. And just to be sure I wouldn't starve, I ordered a side dish of carrots and green beans, with some sorta white sauce drizzled artfully on it.

Pretty as a gallery painting, that meal — but a whole lot more pleasant to eat.

"Might need to stop coming in here," I said halfway through, winking at Wally. "The food's almost as good as my girls cook, but the helpings is double the size I'm allowed, 'cept for when these two need to soften me up and get their own way on something I disagree with."

Wally knew how such banter worked, and joined in the fun right away. He patted his own belly and said, "That's just the *first* reason I'll never marry. I like eatin' whatever I want, whenever I can. No, you won't find me gettin' hitched, not while ever the sun wakes up in the east, and goes for a sleep in the west."

Georgina knew how to play this game herself, and I never *have* knowed a man who could beat a good woman in a battle of wits. "Forgive me for saying so, Wally," she said, looking at him with greatest concern. "But judging by the emaciated state of your torso, it's my strong opinion you've not made good use of your freedom — and indeed, it seems that your ribs make a case for you needing a wife, as it's clear by the way they stick out you're continually forgetting to eat."

True enough, that statement, I reckon. But a'course, I know why young Wally still looks that way now — he's not just a trainer, but a jockey, and must keep his weight down.

He didn't answer with facts though — but instead,

carried on with the game. Could not keep a straight face though, he couldn't, always was a quick one to laugh, young Wally was.

"Ah, that's where you're wrong, Missus Frakes," he began. "See, these big strong ribs a'mine is just what a healthy man needs. So I eat as much as I can manage, but direct all the nutrition to go to my ribs, rather than useless places like ordinary folk. And by the way, Missus, that's some mighty big words you collected to throw at me there — *emaciated* and *torso*. They's real words are they, or did you make them up to flummox poor uneducated folk like myself?"

"Oh, Wally," she answered, busting out laughing. "Please call me Georgina from now on. And if you must know where I found such magnificent words, I get them from Mary, she's the one who collects them."

"Big reader," I added, roughing Mary's hair for her, making her squeal with laughter and drop her fork on the floor.

"Well, Mary," said Wally, after bending to pick up the fork. "You best learn to hold back a few a'them words, else you'll scare all the men, and won't catch one to marry."

"Really?" she asked, fascinated.

"Could be," he said, handing the fork to a waitress and thanking her for bringing a clean one. "Us men ain't mostly clever enough for such words. And contrary-wise, we also like to think *we're* the sharp-minded one, see? Foolish as it may sound, sometimes you might do better to act not so clever as you really are, once you get to an age where boys'll come courting. Then again, pretty thing like yourself, you'll have your pick of 'em all, big words or no, you just wait and see. Ol' Lyle here'll need a big stick to chase 'em all off with."

All a'that pleased Mary no end, but Georgina took it up as a challenge of sorts. Not completely joking she said, "Wally Davis, I like you, I do. But *some* of your opinions are downright boneheaded! Surely a woman's extensive vocabulary can only *entice* the right sort of man. A man who's discriminating and sagacious must *prove* himself to be so, in order to demonstrate himself fit for a clever girl to marry — and vice versa."

"Well, you got me there, Georgina," he answered. "And I reckon you win the argument, for I'm now in agreement."

"You *are?*" She seemed almost disappointed.

"A'course. Why, what you said makes perfect sense. Men and women should just be 'emselves, and that way end up with just the right person that suits ''em, and thusly enjoy their life sentence together, instead a'suffering through it way many folks do."

"Well, quite," she said, though she cocked her head sideways a little, in a show of suspicion.

"Proves *my* point though too," he said — and I thought, *Ha, here we go,* and listened as he went on. "See, Georgina, it proves once and for all that a man like me should *never* marry. Me not understanding even the simplest things about women, or why they cain't just say nothin' at all most the time, like the way horses do. Why, imagine if I married a woman that knowed words like *vocabulary,* and what was that other one you said, some sorta sound like *sagacious! Sa-gay-shuns. Somethin' like that anyways!* Poor simple feller like me would *never* keep up, and just make the poor woman miserable. No, the single life, that's it for me, I *sure* ain't sagacious, *whatever* it means."

It was impressive, way he managed to *almost* keep a straight face til he got near the end — but when he said *sagacious* that last time, he glanced toward me and we both couldn't stand it no more, and Georgina joined in with our laughter.

Then Mary said, "Oh, Mister Wally, sagacious just means intelligent *and* judicious, the two things together."

That's when Wally pressed his hands to his cheeks to hold back his laughter, got himself under control, and said, "Judicious, did you say, Mary? *Judicious?* Are you *sure*, child? I thought I'd seen it *all* in my fifty-three years, but I never knew Jewish folk had their own special dishes. *Jew-dishes.* Well, there's the proof, you learn a new thing every day."

And to little Mary's dismay, we all laughed so hard the waiter had to come over and ask us to hush, as we was disturbing folks trying to eat their own meals.

CHAPTER 24
THE BOOMING SOUND OF A
SCATTERGUN

After we finished eating, we was wandering back up the street, and Wally invited us to go meet his horses. Then he winked at Georgina and added, "My horses being the closest thing a feller like me will get to a wife, I believe you should probably meet them. And that way you'll already be friends with the critters you'll win your fortune on, this coming Saturday."

Mary was so excited we couldn't say no, but Georgina made certain to warn her right off, that we couldn't stay long as racehorses need lots of sleep to perform at their best.

It was a pleasant evening for a walk anyway, and though half the sky was covered with cloud — and we *could* hear a low rumble of thunder quite distant — we knew there wouldn't be no rain to speak of before we got back to our hotel. The moon was more-or-less full, and in the unclouded part a'the sky, at least for the moment.

Real nice evening for taking the air and stretching the legs.

We were still maybe fifty-some yards from Stilson's Livery Stables when we heard a great ruckus erupt there, and Wally took off toward it, putting the licks[1] in.

Plenty to be said for the physical condition of jockeys, if you went by his speed — for I reckon an average man of his age woulda struggled to trot that distance without keeling over.

As he took off, I told my girls "Wait with these folks right here," and nodded toward an old couple who'd opened the door of their bakery to see what was making the ruckus.

I took off after Wally, but my own personal speed is akin to a turtle's — these ol' knees a'mine the main culprit, in addition to a natural lack of ability and too much recent good eating.

I could hear Wally yelling as he raced inside, and the horses was panicked and some mules took up braying, and then just as I got to the doorway there was the booming sound of a scattergun. Well, I ain't a complete fool! I hit the deck and rolled for the safety of a big bag of feed that was right by the table just inside the door.

Rolled right into the leg of the table I did, and a couple of horseshoes tumbled off of its edge, landing right on my foolish old noggin.

I scrambled under the table as my eyes adjusted to the light, and at the open barn doors at the rear of the Livery, the silhouette of a big solid feller hightailed it round the corner and went outta view.

"Good work, Godfrey," called Wally, as he checked out the unconscious stable-boy. "You reckon you got a piece of him?"

I looked up to see the proprietor, Godfrey Stilson, up in his hayloft, still pointing his scattergun at the back doors.

"Reckon not," Stilson said, "but I give him a mighty good scare. I couldn't risk hurting the horses, so I fired at the wall. How's young Cartwright look, Wally?"

Not having met Stilson previous, and not knowing how itchy his trigger finger might be — and him having one barrel left still to fire — I was careful when I made my presence known.

"Wally, tell Stilson who I am now, so he don't fill me with holes."

"It's fine, Godfrey," called Wally, and a good thing it was, for the man had already pointed that scattergun in my direction, awaiting the verdict. "It's just my good friend Lyle Frakes. He's awful slow on his legs, but he came here to back me. Get here, Lyle, quick, the boy's taken a beating. Godfrey, go fetch a sawbones — and hurry, the kid's in a bad way."

I stepped across to where Wally was kneeling, and he sure wasn't wrong — his young stable-boy weren't in good shape. I grabbed a bucket of water and some clean rags from off of the table, and commenced to wipe some of the blood off the young feller's face, to check out the damage underneath.

He was unconscious and then some, his breathing shallow and ragged, and he sorta moaned on the out-breath. Been hit with a shovel was my best guess, as there was a deep cut along the side of his head from a sharp sort of edge, and his eye socket seemed to be busted, and maybe his nose.

Stilson was back with the Doc in under three minutes, and less than a half-minute later the young Sawbones sent him back to his surgery for a stretcher.

"Never thought I'd be a doctor's dogsbody when I opened this place a year back," said Stilson. Then as he trotted off he scolded the gawkers who'd assembled outside his doors looking in, and promised he'd shoot every one of 'em still in attendance when he returned.

By the time he got back with the stretcher, Deputy Emmett Slaughter had arrived, someone having sent word there was shooting at the far end of town.

The young Sawbones — Doc Buckhalter his name was — ordered Wally and Stilson and Emmett and me to carry the stretcher back to his surgery, and I seen Wally's gaze go to the open back doors of the Livery.

I seen right away what the problem was.

"Someone needs to stay here, Doc," I said. "These racehorses has to be guarded, that's why the young feller got attacked. I'll grab another man from outside so one of us can stay here."

There was still a few gawkers outside, though they all hung back on account of the earlier threats made against them. I took a quick look, then chose a big sober-lookin' feller to help with the stretcher.

"You stay here with the horses, Wally," I said, but he wouldn't hear of it.

"It's my fault young John Cartwright got beaten. I

shoulda been *here,* not gallivanting all about town enjoying myself. Can *you* stay, Lyle, please? I need to know he'll be alright."

He sure did look grim as they got the boy on the stretcher and picked it up off the floor. Young Doc Buckhalter led the way without further ado, carrying his doctoring bag out the door, and along the almost dark street.

"There's extra shells for that scattergun there on the table, Frakes," said Godfrey Stilson, looking back at me as they went out the doorway. "Might wish to close the back doors too. No sense taking chances."

I nodded at him and took up the Greener, made my way to the table to load it, then remembered something important.

"Wally," I called, leaning out the front doorway. "If you see my girls, please tell 'em to return to the hotel and wait for me there. I left 'em outside a bakery."

"I'll tell 'em," he called back over his shoulder.

Shotgun in hand, I closed the front doors, then the back ones as well. Weren't no one else gettin' in here.

I sat myself down at the table, and pulled out that damn threatening letter to study it for clues. But a half-minute later, there was a loud knock at the front doors, not three feet away from me. Startled me some, is the truth of it — ain't the jumpy type, me, but engrossed in that damned piece a'paper as I was, I near flew right outta my skin.

"State your business," I called, shoving the note in my pocket as I stood, and taking up the Greener again. "Or I'll fill you with so many holes you'll piss in six different directions."

"Will I *indeed?*" called Georgina. "A *fine* way to speak to your wife!"

I laid down the scattergun, opened the door a little, told her and Mary to get inside quick, which they did.

I checked to see no one had followed, then shut and bolted the door. I looked into Georgina's eyes. "Did Wally not see you?"

"Yes, but he told us to go back to the hotel and—"

"So why the *hell* are you here? This ain't a game, girl. If I say to take the child elsewhere, you need to listen!"

"That's not fair," she replied, gripping my arm.

I unclamped her hand and removed it, walked away from her, silently fuming.

"Mister Wally said the danger was over," said Mary. "We were scared, Father, *please* don't be mean."

I took in a big breath, and it came out twice as loud. *I had overreacted.* I looked at them now, saw my darling Georgina was trembling.

They both of 'em looked white as clean sheets, and I had them sit down while I filled them in best I could.

They had seen young Cartwright up close. Of course it had scared them.

And also, they had not seen the damn letter. I'd best keep it from them.

I calmed my voice best I could and apologized for my short temper. Then I quietly assured them that the boy would most probably live — though he'd sure have himself quite a headache.

"Will he lose his eye, Father?" asked Mary, her voice so concerned that I felt her pain too. "It looked *awfully* bad to me."

The world could be cruel, and the truth of it was, the boy may yet lose more than his sight.

But all the worry in the world wouldn't help him, and my job right now was to stop my child from hurting — even if I had to lie.

"I don't believe his eye is too bad, child. His head was cut deep, and the blood run down into the eye — all that blood made it look worse than it really was. How's about we try and figure out which one a'these horses in here is the fast one, so we can meet it like Wally suggested? Reckon you'll work it out, Miss Mary Frakes. If anyone here knows good horseflesh, I reckon it's you."

---

1. LICKS: To put the licks in is to run (or ride) very fast.

CHAPTER 25

"YOUNG CARTWRIGHT'S SKULL MIGHT BE FRACTURED..."

It was thirty minutes til Wally Davis and Godfrey Stilson returned — by which time Mary had explained in detail just *why* the fast horse was surely the small chestnut mare in Stable Six.

I bet her a dollar, and soon as Wally returned he confirmed I had lost the wager — not with words, but by going straight to the animal to check her in case she'd been injured during the ruckus.

"Doc says poor young Cartwright's skull might be fractured," said Wally as he opened the door to the number six stable. "Reckons the eye will be fine, but he'll have to stay where he is overnight and be taken to hospital tomorrow if he can be moved. Fractured skull or not, he'll need round-the-clock care for a week, maybe two."

"That's a relief," I replied. "It coulda gone worse."

I handed my dollar to Mary without saying a word about bets — though I will say, Georgina looked none too happy about me encouraging the child to gamble.

"Figured she'd lose," I mumbled to my wife, "and that losing would teach her a lesson better than words might."

As Wally's keen eyes and hands examined every part of that small chestnut mare, Godfrey Stilson leaned against a stable railing, thoughtfully chewing on a long piece of straw as he filled us in on what happened.

"I was up in my hayloft having a snooze after dinner," he began, "but being a light sleeper, I woke soon as I heard voices below. At first I wasn't alarmed, the voices not being raised. But as I listened I realized what was happening and my ears pricked up, they sure did."

"Argument?"

"No, Frakes, not that. The stranger was trying to bribe young John Cartwright to throw the upcoming race."

"John's the jockey for the Cup horse, you see," Wally said, examining a forefoot with a magnification glass he'd produced from his pocket.

"I was about to climb down the ladder and throw the snake out, when my own name got mentioned," said Stilson. "Stops a feller in his tracks when he hears his name spoke, such situations. But it was only that young John had told the feller he'd better leave, or Mister Stilson would shoot him right where he stood. But the stranger just laughed, said he knew for a fact I was not here, but in the saloon, same as every night at this hour."

"That usually true?"

"Most usually, yes, but tonight I felt like a snooze, as I'd gotten up early this morning and had no rest all day. Busy time for us liverymen."

"So this stranger must know your habits," Georgina

said. "Perhaps he's not a stranger at all, did you see his face?"

"Or know his voice?" Mary asked.

"Clever child," said Stilson, with a couple of slow nods. "At that point I couldn't see the feller at all. I got a look a bit later, not that it'll help none. He had a hat on, but also he wore a bandana over his face, which muffled his speaking. And I think he'd put on a fake voice — it just sounded wrong to my ears, though I couldn't say why. Anyways, I suspected the man would be armed, so I had to move real quiet to get to Ol' Betsy, other end a'the hayloft from where I'd been sleeping. Foolish of me, that, but we never have trouble in town much, and I was tuckered out, like I said. Guess I didn't think it right through."

My own glimpse of the intruder had been short, and my impressions of him vague at best. But the quicker I asked some questions, the more likely we'd get good answers.

"Color of the bandana?" I asked. "And also his clothing?"

"Like I said before, I couldn't see him at that time. But when I did later, the bandana was black, just like the rest of his clothing. Came dressed for sneaking, I guess, now you ask about colors. Tall heavy-set feller he was, if that's your next question."

All the while Mary had been watching everything Wally did as he checked out the horse. I know she was listening too, as I saw her react to Godfrey Stilson's words once or twice — but her eyes never once got diverted from what Wally was doing.

Stilson took the piece of straw from his mouth now,

looked at it from this and that angle, like as if it might hold the answers to some question he had. But then he threw it to the floor, picked up a fresh one, commenced to chew it as he went on.

"Stranger offered young John three-hundred if he'd throw the race, then upped it to four when John told him to git. Then the feller turned mean, told John if he didn't do it they'd just shoot Light of My Life between now and race day. Told him if he let slip a word of it he'd be killed too. Young John yelled at the feller to git then, and called out to me to wake up. Well, I jumped to it then, and got to Ol' Betsy as quick as I could, but there ain't much headroom up there, so I was a mite slow. I could hear 'em scuffling as John tried to get the better of the man, and I reckon he near had him too from the squeals he made — John was squeezing the man's stones so tight, the feller was blue, and I reckon his..."

Stilson's voice trailed off, and he looked around some alarmed, first at Georgina then Mary. A sort of low groan come out of him then, as he bowed his head and run one of his hands down over his eyes — done that maybe three or four times.

"It's fine, Mister Stilson," said Georgina, kindly and matter-of-factly. "The child *never* listens when there's horses about."

In my opinion, Mary *had* heard it — but she done a good job of *not hearing,* so as not to embarrass the man any worse.

Stilson nodded an apology to me, breathed out one a'them sighs of relief, and went right on with the story.

"I yelled some encouragement to John as I picked up Ol' Betsy, but I sure couldn't shoot, for I woulda killed John too for sure. And besides, at that time John near enough had the feller. Half the man's size, young John was, but he sure has some strength, must be from riding strong horses."

"Ain't the size a'the dog in the fight," Wally said. "And John might be the size of a lapdog, but he's got a huge heart — just like this little horse a'mine, Lulu."

"No argument there," Stilson said, nodding agreement before he went on. "Right there by the table they was, rolling around on the floor, and that masked feller squealing fit to raise up the dead. But right when it seemed like John had him, that slippery snake reached up with his hand and grabbed a broken horseshoe off the table. Clocked poor John with it, he did, right on the noggin. Hit him again and again, then he jumped up and ran — but out the back way for some reason."

"Musta heard me comin' the front way I reckon," said Wally.

"Reckon that'd be it," Stilson said, inspecting his chewed piece of straw a long moment as he nodded agreement. "If he'd gone out the front I'd have got a clean shot. But when he went toward the back doors, there was horses nearby the whole time. So I fired at the wall just to let him know not to come back."

"Well," Wally announced, "Lulu here is just fine, completely uninjured. But now I best check the gelding, then figure out what to do for a jockey. We still gotta win this dang race — we'll win it for John."

CHAPTER 26
JAWING IT OUT

After walking my girls back to our hotel room, I wandered on down to the Sheriff's Office to see if Emmett Slaughter was there.

He was behind his desk, filling out the paperwork on what had happened to young John Cartwright, having only just finished making enquiries around town.

"No clues who it was yet, Deputy Slaughter?"

"Invisible man," he said as I walked in and sat down across from him. "No one saw him walk in, no one saw him run out. *And* no horse galloped away."

"Invisible feller would have an invisible horse," I said. "Stands to logic, don't it?"

"Maybe it does at that," he said with a chuckle, putting the pen in its holder by the side of the inkwell. "Coffee, Lyle?"

"Take a small cup, just to be sociable."

He went over to the stove and poured two cups, brought them back. He sat on the desk while we talked, keeping an eye on the door the whole time. With all the extra visitors in town for the horserace, there was an extra Deputy on duty, and we didn't want anyone hearing what we had to say.

We spoke about how I knew Wally, and I told him I'd been back out to see Delvene Abbott again, but not found out nothing useful.

"We may never solve the Wilson murders," he said. "But at least now we know Henry Abbott was murdered as well — and probably by the same man."

"At some point, Emmett, I'll have to speak some harsh words with Red's brothers, maybe beat the truth from 'em if that's what it takes."

He nodded, slow and thoughtful, and said, "I went over the case files again, and they were the only witnesses to it. All three Abbott boys, Red included. If I'd been here when it happened I'd know more than I do — but there's no way to tell from a written statement if somebody's lying. I guess we're just about at the point where I'll have to speak to them personally — problem is, if the Sheriff *did* cover it up, he'll fire me from my job right away, then I won't have any jurisdiction to investigate further."

"Gettin' fired ain't the worst that might happen," I reminded him, turning to look out the door as a pair of drunks started to argue outside. "If the Sheriff did cover it up — and I reckon he's just the sort — it's likely enough he pulled the trigger himself."

"Your point being, I might be next in line for an accident ... *cleaning my gun.*"

"Or me," I said, taking the threatening letter from where I'd shoved it deep in my pocket.

"What's that?" he asked as I unfolded it and handed it to him.

He lay it out flat on the table, stared at it several moments, then looked up at me.

"Leave Cheyenne or your family die. Was this left at your hotel, Lyle?"

I shook my head. "Restaurant. Girl said they got no idea who left it. They just found it there, no one seen anything. I ain't had a chance to look at it proper just yet, with all that went on since."

Young Emmett turned over the paper, examined the words written on the other side. "Strange, isn't it? To go to the trouble of making the note from newspaper cuttings — yet writing all these words on it in their own hand?"

I read the words out aloud. *"Please hand to Lyle Frakes as accompaniment to his meal tonight."*

"Neat hand, Lyle. Written by a *man* though, I'm certain. Spelling's all correct, too."

"I wondered if it was. Fair size words, this being Cheyenne and not Boston."

We jawed it out a few minutes, but decided, in the end, it was just a complication that we didn't need. Sure, it could be something to do with the murders — but I'm Lyle dang Frakes, and there ain't no shortage of revengers wherever I go. Chances are, it was just some dang fool trying to put the wind up me, on account of me locking them up twenty years ago somewhere-or-other for something I've long forgotten.

We agreed to ignore it for now, and keep our attention where it needed to be — on finding a killer.

CHAPTER 27
THE TEN DOLLAR QUESTION

Me and Emmett drank coffee and talked, then we talked and drank coffee.

We talked probabilities, possibilities, and made our way through unlikelihoods. Seemed like we weren't gettin' nowhere — but we *knew,* the key was the Abbotts.

"Emmett," I said, "let's just assume that Red wasn't just talking a whole load of gibberish while he was dying. That being the case, Henry Abbott's killing *must* be somehow related to horse racing."

"I think I agree, Lyle. Unless the Wilson property has a gold mine on it somewhere."

"In which case they'd a'wrapped up the ownership of it sooner," I said. "Now, Delvene has no idea where their money come from — only that Henry always returned from the East with valuable horses *and* an oversized pile of cash. And each time he went, he took *one* of his sons, but a *different* one every time. Wonder why he would do that —

take a different one every time? There just *might* be something in that."

"Red was dying when I found him, it's true, Lyle. And some of what he spoke *was* gibberish. But mostly he made good sense, and he was clear as could be that there was three murders, and it *wasn't* him or his brothers. And we've *both* met the mother — I've asked around town about her too, just to be sure. By all accounts, Delvene Abbott's as straight as a gun-barrel."

"She's a good woman, no question. And the name Jesse Gillespie meant nothing to her at all — I watched her close when I said the name, and she didn't react. But *her* goodness don't necessarily extend to her sons. This is all about horses and racing, young Emmett. If we find where that money was coming from, we'll find the reason Red Abbott was murdered. And Henry as well."

He nodded slowly — but it was the nod of a man not *quite* in agreement. "But what about the Wilsons? They had no connection with racing at all. How could *they* be involved? It doesn't make sense."

"Might be they *was* mixed up in it somehow. I've questioned Mary — just a little here and there so as not to upset her needless. All she knows is that her parents grew some sheep and some pigs, had a milk cow and chickens, grew extras in their garden to sell a little sometimes. All sounds above board to me — but sometimes even the most honest fellers get tempted and dragged into things that was best left alone. Just makes sense that this is about racing — my money's on some sorta horse-trading thing."

"I'm not saying you're wrong, Lyle, I agree, this

probably *is* about horses. But *if* it is, there's another part to the puzzle — *what* could have gotten the Wilsons caught up in it all?"

"That's the ten dollar question," I replied. "And I been rattling the thought of it round in my head so much it now echoes. So here's the best thought I got — could be that Henry Abbott had Jacob Wilson sell someone a dud horse."

"Possible," Emmett replied from the stove, as he poured us more coffee. He nodded slowly to himself as he spoke, building up the theory in his mind, considering possibilities. "So *maybe* they sold this dud horse to Jesse Gillespie, and he took revenge on the Wilsons — then two days later, he also killed Henry Abbott." Then he stopped, turned to me, shook his head. "But surely if the Wilsons were involved, they'd have had extra wealth to show for it? From all I've heard, they *never* had much, just always barely scraped by."

"There's the rub," I replied. "All they ever had was their land and a humble two-room cabin. A horse or two and a buckboard that barely could make it to town and back without breaking a wheel or axle. And we know he weren't a drunk, as they was Temperance folk."

He raised up his eyebrows. "Didn't know about that. And it *does* raise other possibilities."

I shook my head. "There weren't no other violence against Temperance members round here these few years. A threat here or there, but nothin' more than warm air."

"I agree," Emmett said, placing down his empty cup then stretching his neck side to side before saying, "Killings are *mostly* about money."

"Such small monies as the Wilsons had to spare was all spent on books for young Mary, instead of improving their spread. Good investment, as it turned out. But most folks woulda fixed up their property some. Speaking of which, do you know of a skunk called Orville Lannigan?"

Emmett's eyebrows went skywards some then, and his whole face broke into a smile. "You mean the Orville Lannigan whose *associate* you beat to a pulp in the town's best saloon just two days ago?"

"Weren't hardly beat to a pulp. I just tickled the big feller some when his boss sicked him onto me. Must be tiring, carrying all them heavy muscles around — 'cause he was havin' a little lie down when I left."

"Whatever you say, Lyle. And yes, in fact I *have* heard of Lannigan. The Sheriff's not happy about what you did, and I've heard the names *Lannigan* and *Frakes* again and again these days since — and not in a happy voice either."

"Surely the Sheriff don't think *I* done anything wrong."

"Too many witnesses made statements that said you only defended yourself — you're the talk of the town, in fact. But Mayor Fisk called Sheriff Pettygore to his office, and when the Sheriff came back he was in a mood to kick dogs, I was told. He went off on a rant, *Lannigan this, Mayor Fisk that, and Lyle damn Frakes somethin' else.* Seems Lannigan has powerful friends, like the orphanage man did."

"He'll end up the same way," I said, "if he don't pull in his head. He's been using the Wilson place for his own — built a good corral there to keep a remuda, and been grazing cattle on the place. Lets his cowhands use the home for a bunkhouse — even added a big room onto it."

Emmett stood up and stretched, scratched his chin again. "Interesting," he said, thoughtful-like. "Perhaps *he's* involved in all this. If he wanted the Wilson place and they wouldn't sell..."

"Possible," I agreed. "The damn Mayor weren't too happy when some new feller sent out a demand for the rates to Mavis Benson. Seems ownership of the Wilson place was transferred to the orphanage when Mary moved in there — but Mavis knew nothing of it."

"But if Lannigan was involved in their murders, surely August Benson would have transferred the deed to *Lannigan* soon after it all happened. No, Lyle, I don't think he's part of it. Just a gut feeling, but I think you're on the right track. It's something to do with the horses."

"Careful with them gut feelings, young Emmett. You're already a *good* lawman — you start payin' attention to your guts and your bones, you'll likely turn into a great one, and get yerself packed off to a big city somewhere, to be put in charge of an office."

"No chance of that, Lyle. They'll hear I've been associating with you, and send me right back."

"I sure hope so," I said. "Cheyenne needs at least one honest lawman, and I ain't comin' outta retirement now, I'm too old. Now what are you up to tomorrow? I sent a warning to Lannigan that he'd best be off Mary's place when we arrive to move in. Might be some fun to be had, if he don't comply — you up for the frolic?"

Emmett's eyebrows went upways again, and his whole face broke into a smile. "Wouldn't miss it for the world."

CHAPTER 28
LEAVE OR DIE FRAKES — LAST
WARNING

M e and Emmett changed the time for the move to the Wilson place the following day — Thursday, it would be — so instead of leaving at eleven to get there by twelve, we'd leave just after two. Reason being, to allow the young Deputy a full seven hours of sleep once he finished his night shift.

So, right after breakfast Thursday morning, I wandered on down to see Wally Davis. I was eager to hear how young John Cartwright was doing — but also I wanted to make certain that Wally himself was alright.

Seemed to me Wally might be in danger, though the first attempt to get at his horse ended badly.

Persistent, bad fellers can be, when there's money to be made.

We took a seat on some big bags of feed just inside the Livery doors, and we drank some pretty poor coffee while we had a talk.

All eggshells and just about cold, that dang coffee. Made

with horse-dung and mud, not Arbuckles, in my opinion. Godfrey Stilson mighta cared well enough for his horses, but he's lucky there ain't no law against making bad coffee — if there was, he coulda been hanged, for such swill as he poured us.

Wally told me the boy was out of the woods, and he'd gone down to see him right after he woke, while Godfrey Stilson and Ol' Betsy kept an eye on the horses.

"Not in hospital yet then?" I asked.

"The Doc plans to move the boy to the Hospital later today, now his condition is stable. *Stable*, Lyle. You get it?"

"What?"

"Stable. You know? Horses and *stables*, you see?"

Guess all these problems was weighing on my heavy, and my docity weren't what it should be.

"Good to see you got time for jesting, young Wally," I said. "We need to sometimes, just to keep our worries at bay."

"Good one," he said. *"Bay.* But my horses is chestnuts."

"You got me again," I replied. "I'd only said it on accident, Wally, I ain't clever like you. How's the boy taking it anyway? Must be tetchy as a teased snake."

"I know I would be, but John's more concerned for the horses than for himself," Wally told me. "Fool kid. He's disappointed he can't ride Lulu in the Cup, but he understands he needs to listen to the Doc til he heals."

There was a true hint of pride on Wally's face when he said all that. The stableboy had a love for horses that rivaled his own, and he'd be a fine horseman by the time Wally finished his training.

Thing was, Wally was concerned about how he might keep the Cup horse perfectly safe, knowing the lengths these skunks had gone to to get at her.

"The race is only two days away, but the horses still need some light exercise to keep them in trim — on the other hand, I gotta keep 'em safe from whoever's trying so hard to stop 'em. It's a conundrum alright."

"Quite a mouthful of word, Wally," I said, trying not to laugh. "Co-nun-drum, was it? Best be careful with that one, you might attract the wrong sorta woman, by your own reckoning."

He smiled at the irony of it, then asked if maybe I'd be able to help some — just go with him whenever he took out the horses for their long walks each day.

But I had a better idea.

"You might should come to the Wilson place with us," I told him. "There's stables and yards and good grass, and no one can get near the place without us seeing. Also, it's likely them skunks won't know where you've gone, so we won't have no unwelcome visits. And a'course, we'll go in with you on race day — me and Horse and Gertrude I mean, in terms of protection."

"Might be just the ticket," he replied. "But how far from the racetrack? Can't walk horses too far on race day is all."

"Almost an hour's walk from the racetrack, I guess. Too far?"

"Perfect," he said. "We'll head to the racetrack awhile after breakfast, taking our time. And it'll be good to catch up for a couple of days. Things have been so busy we've hardly had time to talk."

Right on two, Wally shook Godfrey Stilson's hand and thanked him for all he had done, and we walked out into the street, made our way to Roy Grimm's Livery.

Wally walked both his horses, while I walked in front, keeping an eye out for all them things beginnin' with esses — snakes, skunks and sneaks, just to mention the main three.

Godfrey had already delivered all Wally's special horse feed and all of his luggage to Roy's in his buckboard two hours previous — our plan being to not draw attention to the fact that Wally was leaving the town.

To anyone watching, it only looked like Wally and me was taking his horses for their daily exercise, somewhere a little north of town — him and me, along with Horse and Gertrude.

As for Wally's things and our own, they were already packed on a buckboard, which Georgina had driven out of Roy's Livery an hour ago — out the back way, a'course — accompanied by Mary, who was mounted on Dewdrop.

I weren't nohow worried for the safety of my girls, despite the fool letter that got left for me at the restaurant. Cheyenne was busy enough at this hour of the day, and the road from Roy's to Emmett's was all within the town limits — no opportunity for skunks to try nothin', my main meaning.

But in the short time I was gone while I went to meet Wally at the other Livery, and come back, some skunk had left another warning — this time at Roy's Livery, while he was across the street getting some lunch.

"I was only gone five minutes, Mister Frakes," Roy told me. "They musta been waitin' for me to leave, then come in the back way. I thought I'd best show you 'fore I moved it. Stinks don't it?"

We looked down at the part-decayed body of a skunk that had been left just inside the back doors in Roy's absence — it was a real, actual flesh-and-blood animal, not some *skunk-of-a-man,* just to make myself clear.

There had been a note sitting on top of it, weighed down with a horseshoe — and again, the note had been made from newspaper cutouts.

LeAvE oR dIE FrAkeS. LaST wArnINg

"Popular feller you are," Wally said. "I take it the note at the restaurant said much the same thing?"

As Roy picked up the poor dead thing with a shovel and dumped it outside in his fireplace, I said, "You shoulda worked for them Pinkertons, Wally."

"Weren't hard to figure," he replied. "You was in a buster of a hurry to stuff that letter inside your pocket before your wife seen it. I knew it weren't somethin' good. You tell her about it yet?"

"Been too busy," I said. "Truth is, I figured that'd be the only one, and there'd be no problem. This changes things some, I guess."

Roy came back inside, said, "You worried about your family, Mister Frakes?"

"Not for the moment, young Roy. We'd have heard a ruckus if anything happened between here and the Slaughter place. Mary's armed and well trained, she'd take some stoppin' alright. By the way, you two ain't met proper yet, have you? Roy Grimm, Wally Davis. Two young fellers with plenty in common."

They shook hands and spoke a little about Wally's chances of winning two races this coming weekend, and it was a pleasant conversation.

Not enough to keep my mind off the threats I'd been getting, which I'd now moved from my *Don't Much Matter* part a'my brain to the *Maybe Worth Payin' Attention To* section.

I'd best give it some thought later on.

Now, although Roy Grimm had never met Wally before, he sure knew of Wally's reputation as a top horseman. Real respectful he was, not surprising — but Roy's eyes kept a'wandering down to the rear of Wally's horse — not the Cup horse, but the other one. Tall young gelding it was, powerfully built he was too.

Wally didn't miss what was happening. "You see something, don't you, young feller?"

"Aw, I don't know, Mister Davis. It ain't nothin' a finger could touch, but there's somethin' about how he's standing. Is he always a picayune off square that way, or is there maybe some little soreness? Near fetlock maybe?"

"I checked him over last night, but I'll look again, Roy," Wally said. "Now you say it, he's maybe a smidgin off somewhere there."

"Might be nothin' at all, Mister Davis. You'd know better than me."

Wally ran a hand over the fetlock, but only shook his head. "No heat or swelling, but I'll take him for a short canter once he's warmed up, check him out after that, and again when he cools."

We said our goodbyes, and while Wally said nothing particular, I could tell that Roy had impressed him.

We rode out of town, keeping an eye out for undue attention, and all met up at Emmett Slaughter's place without incident. We then proceeded together to the Wilson place — but not before having a cup of Jeanie Slaughter's coffee, and one of her tasty biscuits, to keep up our strength.

Never go to war with an empty belly, my Pa used to say. And while this might should go peaceful, you can never be certain when a skunk like Orville damn Lannigan's somehow involved.

CHAPTER 29
"HE TOLD US TO BURN THIS HOWSE DOWN..."

The day was cool, the sun breaking through heavy cloud here and there, just enough to remind us how lucky we are to live in the West, with our good clean air and our freedoms. Along the parts of the trail that had trees both sides, twittering birds flitted from branch to branch, so small and so quick we could not be sure what they were.

A mighty fine day to be alive — and though we was aware there could be some trouble when we arrived, I could see every one of us was enjoying the journey to get there.

None of us really believed there would be any trouble, but as we talked we made a plan for that, just in case.

Many a time I'd have been killed for sure, if it weren't for a Just-In-Case plan.

I still didn't mention them *letters of warning* to the girls — no sense worrying them needless, and we had enough things to be alert on already.

Georgina and Mary weren't happy, as usual, when I

told them they'd have to hang back a few minutes, and let us three men ride in without them.

But they calmed down quick when Wally explained how important their job was, and the reason it had to be done.

"It's these two horses of mine needs protecting, you see? I can't have them exposed to gunfire two days out from a race. I'm trusting you ladies to the most important job of all. You'll need to mount up on them, stand away from anything they might run into if they panic, and keep them both quiet so they don't get hurt."

Mary looked mighty chuffed, but Georgina had reservations. "Are you certain Mary will be strong enough to handle a thoroughbred in race condition?"

Wally gave Mary a confident nod and a wink and said, "I been watching how she handles Dewdrop. Girl's a natural, just like Lyle says. Let's lift her up on the big horse, he's the quieter of the pair."

Made for a comical sight, that small girl on that overtall horse — like a kitten on a buffalo, she looked. But no one said nothing about it, and we all hid our smiles.

We left them in a small clearing at the top of a rise, where they could see anyone coming for at least a half-mile every direction.

"You see anyone, Mary," I said, "don't take 'em on. Just ride down to us, we'll handle it with rifles."

Me and Emmett rode down the hill on our horses, with Wally driving the buckboard behind, all three of us with full-loaded guns at the ready.

For a minute I thought we was headed for trouble, as

the first thing we seen when we came into view of the place was some smoke from the chimney. But there weren't a single horse left in the yards; the gate was latched and unbroken; and indeed the whole place had been left in perfect condition.

"Half-expected they'd vandalize the house," Emmett said as we rode through the entry and up the drive. "But it all looks fine at this distance. We'd best reserve judgment until we're inside, but it looks like nobody's here, and they've left it the way that they should have."

He was right to think that way. Sure, it woulda been too much work to pull down all them good fences they'd built — but I sort of expected the room they had added to the home to be damaged somehow.

We stepped down onto the ground, tied the horses to the porch rail, listened for any wrong sounds.

All as it should be.

Still, we stayed watchful while checking the outbuildings — the original barn was smallish and sturdy, but the new one was a surprise, with quality stables built in it and big doors that locked. But there weren't no other surprises — no one was lying in wait, and every single thing had been left clean and swept out and undamaged.

"Look at this," Wally said when we finally entered the house.

He was holding a note at arm's length, and by the degree of his squinting, could not make out the words.

"Give it to young Emmett," I told him. "I ain't got my eyeglasses with me, and by the looks, you're blinder than I am, young Wally."

"You're the only person I know who still calls me young," Wally said with a chuckle as he handed the paper to Emmett. Then he shook his head slowly and laughed again as he said, "I'm fifty-three years of age, Lyle — an old codger like you. *Young, what a thing to be called.* Anyway, what's it say, Emmett?"

Nothing wrong with Emmett's eyes, he didn't even bother to take the note to the window to get more light on it.

"Ain't another damn warning, is it?" I said. "If it is, I'm gonna find out who sent it, stick it over the end of my gun-barrel, and shove it so far up his—"

"Calm down, Lyle," said Wally. "Folks who write warning notes wouldn't bother to put a posy of wildflowers in a cup on top of the note."

"True enough," I agreed. *Them damn notes was gettin' to me, I guess.*

"I'll just read it out loud, exactly as written," Emmett said, then cleared his throat before he began.

This is the letter he read out to us.

Mr Frakes.

Wen I told Mr Lannigan yore message he got reel angry and told us to burn this howse down so you cant moove in.

We aint the sort that wants trubbel. So me and my 3 frends went to town for a drink and to think about leeving. In town we herd for our selfs wot you dun to Littel Wayne. We respeckt that. A lot.

So we came back and sleeped hear and today we

mooved on back home. Mr Lannigan is a bad one and we aint gunna get jailed for him.

Pleese dont tell him we went back to Kansas wen he gets back from Denver.

We cleened the place best we can. We left the stove burning so you could rassel up sum coffee wen you get hear. Its a good place. We hope you and yore wife and child will be happy hear.

Bert Stone.

And frends.

PS. You shood bet on the horse he bets in the Cup. We herd him speecking to the Mare and the Mares horse will win. But we aint herd its name yet and its sum sort of seecret.

Bert Stone.

And frends.

CHAPTER 30
IN YOUR BLOOD

The rawboned young cowhand's letter sure raised some questions.

Deputy Emmett Slaughter smiled and raised up his eyebrows. "I'll make a report about this, and it'll be enough that I'll get to warn Lannigan to keep away from you. Not just that either — I'll let him know that if *anything* untoward happens here, I'll charge *him* with it, and the Judge will be shown the letter, and all four witnesses brought to testify that *he* said to burn the place."

"I don't know, Emmett," I said. "Young Bert Stone done the right thing, and he only asked we don't let Lannigan know where he went. You file that report and the Sheriff will tell the damn Mayor, and he'll tell Lannigan."

Emmett smiled a wise one and said, "As it's *you* who actually owns the letter, Lyle, it's *you* who gets to keep it. My report will say that I only saw the start of the letter. The part where Lannigan ordered his men to burn the house down, and that's why they left."

"Careful, Emmett, you sound like a proper lawman, you'll get yourself in trouble."

"I'll go fetch your family," said Wally, and he wore a mighty broad smile. "Not just them a'course. I gots to go get my horses — *including* the one who's gonna run second to the Mayor's horse in the Cup race!"

"Before you go, Wally," Emmett said. "I never knew the Mayor owned a racehorse. And I'm not sure how much Lyle's told you, but we've developed an interest in both those two things of late."

"Oh, he owns a couple alright, but it's a recent hobby, from what I could tell you. Though I've only come back to racing quite recent myself — took a break for three years. Gets in your blood, you see, and always drags you back in. But I can tell you this — the horses he's had running recent ain't worth a stamp. No good for racing at least, though they both *are* good lookers."

"You know his horses then?" I said.

"Sure I do, they's both entered in the Cup Saturday. Waste of the entry fee in my estimation, but hardly surprising — a local Mayor often likes to have his horse in the top race, just to boast of it, see? But both horses ran poorly in easier races last week over in Sidney, when we won the Cup there. I'd best go fetch the animals now, they need to be watered and settled down into the stables."

As Wally walked out I started to follow, but Emmett grasped me by the arm, said, "Let him go by himself, Lyle, if that's alright. Gives us five minutes in private to discuss this new information."

I stuck my head out the doorway and told Wally to take

Horse to fetch them, as me and Emmett had something we had to discuss.

We discussed it alright — young Emmett bouncing ideas off the walls as he spoke rapidfire, and me trying to keep up with his questions and work out where his thinking was going. But in that next few minutes, we managed to work some things out, get 'em clear in both our understandings.

First thing, the Mayor owning racehorses *might* just tie him to the murder of Red, and maybe the Wilsons.

Second thing, we shoulda asked Wally who trains the Mayor's horses.

Third thing — and Emmett looked at me worried when he brought up the subject — why hadn't I yet asked Wally if he knew of a feller who used the name Jesse Gillespie?

I did explain to Emmett that, while I *am* gettin' on, I'm not losing my marbles *completely* just yet. Thing was, I'd been waiting to get Wally on his own before asking all my questions related to racing, as I didn't like to upset young Mary any more than was necessary. And with everything that happened in town — the bashing of the stableboy, mostly — me and Wally had barely had two minutes together where we weren't flat out figuring out other things.

"Soon as they get here," I said, "we'll leave the girls to set up the house, and we'll talk to Wally while we all attend to the horses."

By then they was coming up the drive on them three spirited animals — not racing *exactly,* but they made for a beautiful sight as they loped along easy.

Best of all, ol' Horse seemed to think he was some sorta

racehorse, way he strode past the others to finish a half-length in front with his big easy stride.

"You didn't win that time, Mary," I said with a laugh, as they all pulled up. "Ol' Horse can be hard to beat when he gets a fair start and nobody cheats him."

I helped Mary down off that big gelding and led him away, following Wally. And I called back over my shoulder to Georgina, telling her the young cowhand's letter was inside on the table, and that she was right to talk to him kind, how she did.

"Decent young feller after all," I said.

But when she answered, "What a surprise, fancy me knowing best," I pretended I hadn't heard, and just smiled to myself.

Thing is, us men all learned long ago that our women knows best — but it's better we don't admit it too often, or we'd never get to make *any* decisions for ourselves. And if *that* was the case, how would we ever learn *anything?*

Point being, people learn from mistakes — and us men, we make plenty of 'em.

Just ask any woman alive, and she'll make you a list.

CHAPTER 31
THE MYSTERY OF JESSE GILLESPIE

I 'll say one thing for that Lannigan skunk — he had not skimped on the building of some quality stables in this big barn. Musta had some big plans for this place, I wouldn't reckon.

All store-bought lumber it was, and sanded down smooth. No chance of splinters in here, not for beast nor man neither. Hadn't been too long built, you could still smell the fragrance of the pine. Barn was painted on the outside, a'course, but the inside left natural — just how I like it.

Must thank that skunk Lannigan sometime, and laugh in his dung-eatin' face.

As we watered the horses and settled them into them big roomy stables, some interesting things came to light.

First thing being, it was the Abbott boys who was training the horses owned by Mayor Reginald Fisk. Me and Emmett went quieter than a boneyard at midnight when Wally said it — and after a second or two, he looked up from what he was doing to check why we'd gone so silent.

"Does that mean something important?"

"Could say that, Wally," I replied. "See, two years back, right here somewhere on this one-sixty, Mary's parents were murdered. We're just lucky she weren't here too."

"Poor little chickabiddy. I didn't know," Wally said, and looked around like as if he was wondering where exactly it happened.

Emmett explained, "Report states the bodies were found out front of the house — but then, that report may yet be a load of corral dust and cow-dung. The Sheriff may yet be in on it. Certainly, he sent me and all the other Deputies out to kill Red Abbott some weeks back, after he himself had shot him at their Livery. Sheriff said he shot Red in self-defense, but the truth is, Red was unarmed."

"Red was Delvene's other son," I explained.

"Interesting," Wally said, going back to his work. "You shoulda asked me about all this sooner. Even though I've been away from racing awhile, I have friends we can talk to." Then as if he was reading our minds he added, "And my friends can be trusted not to share what I've asked them — both with lawmen *and* damn politicians."

Young Emmett — being a lawman himself — raised his eyebrows and smiled a wry one, but Wally missed it, as he was running a hand over that tall horse's fetlock, slowly, deliberately, feeling for the slightest bit of swelling or heat.

So Emmett just winked at me and said, "How well do *you* know the Abbotts, Wally?"

"I don't know the boys more than to say howdy —

couldn't even tell you their names. I knew Henry and Delvene good enough to have an opinion. That opinion being, Delvene is the salt of the earth, and as straight as they come. But Henry ... how should I put this? Never speak ill of the dead, and all that — but it wouldn't overstate things to say he was easily led, and always open to making a quick buck. On the good side, he sure could keep his mouth shut — which was why, even though he mighta skated sometimes on thin ice, he never found himself in no trouble."

"Until he did," I pointed out.

Wally placed the horse's hoof on the floor and looked into my eyes. "Yes. He wasn't a man to die cleaning his gun. Henry was careful and clever. Everything he did was thoughtfully planned, and he never made many mistakes."

"Until he did."

They both nodded in agreement, then Emmett said, "One other thing, Wally. While poor Red was dying — *awful thing* — he gave me the name of the man who murdered Henry Abbott and the Wilsons. But here's the thing — there's no record of such a man anywhere, so we figure it must be an alias."

"Plenty of those in the racing game. Run it by me, I might know of the feller."

"When Red was dying, he told me the killer's name was Jesse Gillespie. That ring any bells?"

Wally sorta half-smiled, looked from Emmett to me, searched my eyes. Seemed like he thought we was making a joke, but I guess he found nothing but puzzlement in my eyes — for the smile drained away from his face, and it seemed like his thoughts darted every which way then.

"Jessy Gillespie," he said, slowly shaking his head, like he thought we was loco. "Red told you that *Jessy Gillespie* killed two men and a woman?"

"He *was* a bit of a mess at the end — but yes, that's what he said, and I *do* believe him." Emmett drew in a sharp breath of anticipation, glanced my way a second, then looked back and added, "So, Wally? You *do* know the man then?"

"No," Wally answered. "I don't know the *man*. Because Jessy Gillespie's a filly. J. E. S. S. Y. Jessy with a Y. She's a filly."

The shock of it shook me, I'll tell you. "A *woman?* A *woman* gunned down Mary's parents? I cannot believe such a thing."

"Not a *woman*," said Wally. "A filly. A real, actual, flesh-and-blood *filly*. Or rather, she *was* back when she was well known — she'd be a mare now, you see, if she's still alive. She'd be six years old."

Emmett wore a look of bewilderment, so I explained, in case that was why. "Female horse is a filly til she turns four," I said, "then she's a mare."

A strange look came over Wally's face then — no stranger than the one Emmett wore — and Wally said, "What *exactly* was it that Red said? Because now I think on it some, it seems like a wild rumor I heard might yet turn out to be true."

And right then, Emmett Slaughter proved once again what sort of a lawman he is. He said, "I was wrong all this time. But we'll get to the bottom of this yet. Do you feel it, Lyle? It's coming together, it's coming."

He pulled some notes from his pocket.

And before I could ask what they were, I already knew. It was the notes he made soon as Red died. *He had brought them along, knowing they might come in handy when he spoke to Wally.*

"A horse," Emmett said with excitement, as he unfolded the notes, laid 'em out flat on a workbench, and smoothed the wrinkles out from 'em. His voice then took off at fifteen to the dozen — I never heard him talk so fast in the time that I've knowed him.

"Wally, how did you know the horse right away, just like that, and what was the rumor? And let me look at these notes to see where I went wrong. A horse, she's a horse, Lyle, we're gonna get 'em, I feel it all through my bones now! We're *sure* gonna get 'em, and send 'em to prison, or string 'em all up, which is just what those snakes all deserve!"

"He often speak that fast?" said Wally.

"Just when he feels things in his bones, would be my guess."

Wally shook his head slowly, tapped himself on the noggin several times as he said, "Glad I ain't got such bones — this ol' upper storey a'mine would never keep up."

CHAPTER 32
"PA DONE THE DYING..."

"Look here," Emmett cried then, running a finger down the paper to point at one thing then another. "Of *course!* Red was telling me things as fast as he could, but I foolishly kept asking questions, and taking what he next said as the answers. I should have shut up and listened, instead of confusing him worse how I did."

Me and Wally looked over his shoulder, but without my glasses, I couldn't read anything anyway.

Wally squinted his eyes up and said, "You must have some mighty fine peepers, young Deputy Emmett, why is it writ all so small? You best read it out loud, and maybe between all us three we can piece the true meaning of it all together."

Emmett read out the words on the paper, and when he said *'walnuts'* Wally said, "Hmmm, that fits with the rumor, go on."

Emmett read out a few other things, then he said, "Pa done the dying. Big money. Jesse Gillespie."

That's when Wally Davis jumped in the air like a young stallion, cried out, "It was true, the dang rumors was true, blow me down with a feather! No wonder they wouldn't sell her to me, they had some mighty big plans! Jessy Gillespie!"

His hat had fell off when he started his jumping, so I picked it up, hit it once against my leg to remove any dust, and handing it to him I said, "Must be *some* rumor. Secret is it? Or do you plan to share it with the rest of us?"

"It sure *was* a secret," he told us, "and a pretty well kept one, as secrets go. Secret like that gettin' out could get a man killed."

"Seems to me like it did. Three men and a woman, perhaps, and we're maybe still counting."

Wally blew out a breath. "We gotta be careful, lest they add *us three* to the tally. Don't say nothing to Georgina and Mary, not yet at least anyway. Here's what happened."

"Can't wait to hear it. Hows about we sit down a spell?"

Emmett sat himself on the workbench, while I sat on the chair that had been underneath it. As for Wally, he was currying his horse the whole time he spoke.

"Jessy Gillespie was a pretty top horse," Wally said, his voice all admiration. "Lotta folks expected she'd win the Kentucky Oaks as a three-year-old — me included — but she got injured in running and finished near last. It was a muscle tear in her near shoulder, you could see the swelling as soon as they brought her in off a'the track. She wouldn't be able to race at the top level again, not after that muscle tear. I tried to buy her to breed with right away, and they said *Maybe, we'll think on it a week, let you know.* A week later they said *No.* I made a bigger offer, a'course — huge money it was, but they turned it down flat."

"So she couldn't run any more," Emmett said. "But what does this have to do with walnuts?"

"A horse can still *gallop* when that muscle heals," Wally explained. "On a left-turning track she'd be about six lengths slower than she was before. Just a slight loss of speed, but less balance on the turns, you see? So even a top horse like her can't win the *big* races. But a country race like the ones around here, a quality horse like Jessy Gillespie would win such a race in a romp. And you'd have to take it easy on the work, only gallop her sparing-like, only race her once every blue moon."

Emmett looked at him sideways like a poor confused pup. "I'm still not with you, Wally."

"The first clue's the walnuts. The second's in what you wrote down, what Red said of his Pa. Only listen to the words, and ignore what you first thought they meant."

Emmett read it out again. ""Pa done the dying. Big money. Jesse Gillespie."

"The walnuts are for dyeing the horse another color," I said, as it finally washed over my poor slow old noggin. "Red's Pa done the dyeing ... *with walnuts.*"

"It's the husk," Wally said. "Inner part a'the peel, outside the nut. Used to stain wood, clothing ... and hair. Been used for thousands a'years, I read once in a book."

"So Jessy Gillespie?"

"Rumor was, she was used as a ring-in quite awhile back, out in San Francisco. Only one feller told me it, and swore me to secrecy, but he died not too long after. Hmmm, now I wonder if ... hmmm. He told me the horse in question had overlong ears, if you can believe it."

"That some sorta code?"

Wally smiled and nodded. "No, it just means what it means. See, every good racehorse has one thing that shows it ain't perfect. When you find one looks perfect, every real good horseman knows that one won't be a winner. Top horse needs something unusual, see? My Lulu, she's tiny, but with an over-wide chest. In Jessy Gillespie's case, it was her big ears."

Made sense to me, so I nodded for Wally to go on, which he did, no delay.

"Anyway, there was a horse that kept finishing near to last in her races — *her name was Thunder Cloud, actually, now I remember* — then suddenly she won a big Stakes race in San Francisco. Just over two years back, this was. And what with all the gold around then, the betting was *huge*. That poor-performed horse won the race, and the bets took a hundred-thousand out of the bookmakers' bags there. Then the horse disappeared, never raced again, couldn't be found."

"Just over two years ago," Emmett said, gripping me by the forearm. "Jessy Gillespie, all the money the Abbotts were making, the dyeing. But how were the Wilsons involved? And why *was* Henry Abbott killed?"

"Anything else we misunderstood on them notes?" Wally asked, his eyes like two shining dark gemstones.

Emmett read out some more. *"The mare! The mare!* Well of course, he meant Jessy Gillespie when he said that."

"Wait up, Emmett," I said. "What else might *the mare* mean? I remember, you told me you'd asked him who'd pulled the trigger, and *'The mare'* was his answer to that. And then you asked *'What mare?'* and he said—"

"Our mare!"

"Exactly," I said. "It ain't *mare* he was saying, but *Mayor."*

And together we both said, *"Our* mayor, the Mayor of Cheyenne. Mayor Reginald Fisk!"

As we jawed on it further, we sorta worked out a plan of what we would do — and just as important, what we *wouldn't* do.

Regarding Georgina and Mary, we decided not to tell them what we'd found out just yet. It could only put them in danger — and Mary in particular could not be expected to keep her temper when she next saw Mayor Reginald Fisk.

I'll have enough trouble myself.

Last thing we needed was for Mary to take out her Derringer and use it on Fisk in front of a whole town of witnesses. That could only end badly.

But we all agreed, she was *entitled* to put a bullet through that bad skunk.

Even Wally's bones felt it, he had to admit — the Mayor *had* killed Mary's parents, there wasn't no doubt.

The problem, as Emmett pointed out pretty quick, was not in the knowing, but the *proving*.

Thing was, if we got half the truth out, and could charge them all with the ring-in, the prosecutor would offer the Abbott boys lighter sentences to tell the whole truth, all about who killed who, and why.

Emmett had plans to look through all the records — it might take several days, as he'd have to be mighty careful the Sheriff didn't find out, or the game would be up. But the young Deputy strongly believed the records would somehow help bring the whole thing together.

But with many more years of Sheriffin' under my belt, I was more pessimistic.

"We'll have to get the Mayor to admit it," I said, "or catch the skunks in the act if they try to do another big ring-in, and that ain't so likely."

"Ain't it?" said Wally, as he rubbed the tall gelding's fetlock with some sort of vinegar mixture, over and over. "You heard what the young cowhand wrote in his note, or are you gettin' forgetful in your old age, Lyle?"

Emmett's smile grew from the middle, and spread out all over his face. "The Mayor told Orville Lannigan he was sure to win the big Cup race."

Wally looked up from his horse and he nodded. "And both of his horses can't run outta sight in a storm. They got a better horse they plan to bring in disguise, or my name ain't Wally Er ... well, never mind what my whole name is, they're up to shenanigans, you mark my words."

It was too much to hope they were foolish enough to bring Jessy Gillespie herself to the race, not after all that happened. But the air fairly bristled with our hopes of it.

"I know what you're thinking," said Wally, "but I don't

like the chances. After a big ring-in comes off, the horse they used for it is usually never seen again — and it was a *huge* ring-in, the biggest I know of in years."

I could sorta picture the two horses the Abbott boys had at the track when Georgina spoke to them — but not well enough to be certain, so I asked the question. "Is one of their Cup horses a mare?"

"Yes, one is," Wally answered, "and the other's a gelding. Mare has similar coloring to Jessy Gillespie, in fact, but has white forelegs and other small differences too. And smaller ears, a'course. And it *has* been long enough they just might think they're in the clear."

"Sounds like a good chance to me."

"Perhaps, Lyle," he said. "But what usually happens, soon as a big ring-in's over, they get rid of *both* horses. And this case is worse, there being murders of people involved, not just horses. Filthy damn skunks, they'll have killed that wonderful horse, as well as them people."

"Jacob Wilson must have been involved somehow," said Emmett. "He must have known something he shouldn't. If only I'd been here back then, might have noticed *something* about him."

"Whatever he done," I said, "he paid a terrible price."

Wally placed the horse's foot on the ground again, turned toward us and nodded his agreement. "We need to catch these skunks out somehow, so they never can do it again — to horses *or* people."

We heard a door bang closed in the distance, and looking out we saw Mary head into the yard and start walking toward us.

"It all seems so small now," she called, waving her hands about. "I used to think it was a mile to our little barn there, yet it's barely forty yards from the house. And *that* seems to have shrunken some too, though it's *actually* bigger with that big extra room."

She looked so tiny, so brave, and I knew that whatever happened I had to protect her, as long as I could stay alive to do so.

"How you doing, child? I asked her, it only now having occurred to me that she might be awful upset, being back where her family was killed.

She shrugged her shoulders and smiled a half-happy, half-sad sorta smile, then ran the rest a'the way and hugged me a moment. Then she looked up and said, "It's sad, of course, but also nice to be home. And though I lost two lovely parents, I'm certain they're both very happy to see I have two wonderful *new* parents now."

"That's a real nice thing to say, child. And you sure know how I feel." As she unwrapped herself from my torso, and took my hand instead, I sniffed just a little and wiped some dust outta my eyes with my free hand.

"I can *feel* their presence here, you know."

"That a fact, child? I bet they can feel yours too."

She smiled at the thought of it and said, "Mother sent me to fetch you all in for some afternoon tea. Apple pie, just *smell* the cinnamon! Oh, and Mother just *loves* the house, and she says those cowhands were nice boys, picking us flowers and thoughtfully heating the stove to welcome us — *however,* their cleaning skills were *deplorably* lacking. Still, we've made a good start while we baked."

"You go start without me," said Wally. "I gots to finish rubbing the soreness outta this fetlock. That young Roy Grimm sure does know his horses. I would not have found it myself til tomorrow, then it would have been too late to fix it in time for the race. I'll be there in five minutes, child, I promise — just don't let old Lyle eat up my share, we all know what he's like whenever there's good pie around!"

CHAPTER 34
CRESCENDO

Our first days and nights at the Wilson place went by mostly quiet and happy. Some rain settled in that first night, the tin roof Jacob Wilson had built not only keeping us dry, but making our lives all the richer with its pleasant sound. The rain met it gentle at first, then rose to a mighty crescendo of *'magically musical magnificence'* — at least, that was how Mary put it, and nobody argued.

Wally slept out with the horses a'course — I didn't waste my breath trying to change his mind on it. Once a horseman always a horseman — and considering recent events, even Georgina and Mary had no valid reason why Wally should not guard his horses every minute.

I left Horse loose the whole time anyway — better than a watchdog, that animal, and twice as good-looking. But no-one gave us cause for alarm.

Not yet anyway.

Seemed too easy almost — as if no-one had cottoned on

to where Wally had gone, or noticed us Frakeses missing from around town.

Truth is, the quietness made me uneasy.

Still, life has a way of making things interesting, and the biggest storms usually follow the quietest times.

Reckon that might should be a saying, and writ up in books.

Perhaps folks figured Wally was keeping his horses confined to Stilson's Livery, only bringing them out at the most ungodly hours of the night for a small bit of exercise. Perhaps whoever left them threatening letters just don't yet know where to deliver 'em. *Guess we'll find out soon enough.*

Wally worked on getting them horses trained to the minute, and taught Mary all manner of things as he did.

As for me, I did a few things about the place, but by the middle of Friday afternoon I felt like a caged lion, and needed to do something more than oil hinges and put a fresh coat of paint on the outhouse — which, I might add, it didn't actually need.

"Might go for a ride," I told Georgina, as I washed up my coffee cup for the *sixth* time that day. "It's Horse," I explained, "he gets nervy when there ain't much to do."

She bit her lip how she does, smiled one a'them knowing smiles a'hers, and asked me where I planned on going.

"Might drop by the Abbott place. Got a question or two for Delvene."

"Good idea," Georgina replied. "Whatever it is you and Wally are keeping a secret, you'd best get more information about it before race day tomorrow if possible."

She knows we know something. Well a'course she does.

"Always could read me like a book, couldn't you, Princess? You know I'll tell you when the time's right?"

"I know," she said. "And I trust you to handle it your way. I'm just glad Wally's here with those horses to keep Mary distracted, or she'd know how close you are too. Let me know if I can help. Go on, get out of here, you're wearing a track in the floorboards, pacing up and down in that manner. Just don't go near the Lannigan ranch."

"Other direction," I told her.

I kissed my beautiful wife goodbye and told Mary and Wally I was going out for a quick ride. To be honest, I felt a touch miffed when Mary didn't ask to come with me — but I guess ten-year-old girls is more interested in learning how to make up a poultice to treat a horse's sore muscles, than to ride around with their fathers. At least, this *particular* ten-year-old finds the poultice more interesting.

And Wally would be leaving soon — it was a real good thing she could spend some time with the greatest horseman I've known. Not to mention, he's also as good a *man* as you'd meet, a real top-shelf feller, young Wally.

Me and Horse moseyed on out nice and slow, how we do, and even mostly at walking pace we was sitting on the rise looking down on the Abbott Ranch only twenty minutes later.

Problem was, there was visitors there. I stepped down off of Horse, took my spyglass out of the saddlebags and had a slow thorough look.

It was only one of Red's brothers — just him alone, visiting his mother.

I considered riding on down there, and when I weighed up the reasons to, I just about persuaded myself it was a good idea.

I'd be introduced as an old friend and new neighbor, and the young feller might just share some useful information.

But my next thought was, *Ha, Lyle Frakes, you'd tell yourself anything to get something happening quicker. You'd ruin the thing, rushing in like a young bull.*

Because, the truth of it was, the Mayor woulda told them two boys to keep well away from me. After we visited him with Mavis Benson — and also my little frolic with Orville Lannigan's musclebound protector — the damn Mayor would be well aware that I was Mary's new father.

And fathers being protective of their children, it would stand to reason — even to a bad skunk like him — that I would be trying to find out who killed the Wilsons.

Go home, Lyle, go home.

I looked at the ground — the smell of that lovely damp dirt just as sweet to my nostrils as good cherry pie. It had been moistened right through by the rains we'd just had these two days, but not so much as to be heavy — and these backtrails between the Abbott Ranch and the Wilson place was not much traversed by wagons, and therefore not rutted most places.

"Ground's soft and yielding, Horse, just right for old bodies — what's your thinking on enjoying ourselves?"

Old showoff nodded his head, reared just a little to let

me know he was more ready than I was, and we turned and headed for home.

We sure blew out the cobwebs, me and ol' Horse, that whole distance home, like a real pair of youngsters.

Barely five minutes since I said *GO,* we thundered down the last slope, skidded around the tight turn, accelerated through the gateway and up the drive. We was covered in dirt sweat and grime, a good pair of mud-runners showing their speed — not to mention some stamina — and though five minutes ain't exactly *thoroughbred* speed by the clock, it weren't none too shabby for an old pair of poorly bred beasts like him and me.

CHAPTER 35

MARY, SOME SNORING, SOME SNEAKING

Hello again, Mary Frakes here.

Or Mary Frakes-Farmer-Wilson, as I sometimes think of myself — even though the names are chronologically reversed.

Before telling you my part in this story, I must say, my recent time in Cheyenne has been *quite* overwhelming to *all* of my feelings — especially now I've come home to where I lived with my original parents.

I've felt overwhelmed by both the *ecstatic* and the *melancholy* too, in case that wasn't clear.

To see my old home again — as *small* as it now somehow seems, compared to what I remember — has reminded me of *so* many things I'd completely forgotten.

I see my mommy, my daddy too at odd times, just as if they truly are here. And the boundless *joy* that sight brings is quickly replaced by a sadness, as their faces fade into the ether — and I'm left with the knowledge that it was only my overly vivid imaginings, playing tricks on my wishful mind.

Why, even an image of our horse came to mind once. Stranger still, this happened when I walked into the *new* barn — I say *strange,* because that big barn is *new.* It didn't even *exist* when I lived here before.

And also, the horse I mistook for our old one — Mister Wally's mare, Lulu, whose race name is *Light of My Life* — is not *nearly* so large as *our* lovely big mare was.

She was so pretty, that horse, and *magical* too, if you can believe it! I wonder where she is now. I *do* hope she's doing well. She was really quite lovely.

Daddy bought her quite cheaply, and we were *very* excited at our sudden good fortune — up until then we'd had only a mule, a most stubborn beast who seemed *never* to do what we wanted him to.

But our mare had a *beautiful* nature. I was *ever* so fond of her, though we only owned her a few weeks before my dear parents were ... well, let's not talk about *that* any more for the moment.

It was a tragedy, and always will be. And I don't believe we are meant to "Forget It," as some people tell us we should.

It still hurts, and I won't just "Forget It."

How could I?

Why would I?

That mean orphanage owner, Mister Benson, was quite wrong to say it, and I'm glad he's dead, he was wicked!

But enough of bad things! My life is now *wonderful* too, in so many ways. My new mother and father are a gift I will be ever grateful for. And in my heart, I know that somehow, my first parents steered me toward them — *there are things in our lives that are just MEANT to be, and it's best to not overthink them, but remember to be grateful.*

And I am — I truly AM grateful for all that I have.

Oh dear, I'm so sorry, I *quite* forgot to go on with the story! Something *very* important has happened, and I *should* have told you already! Well, here it is now!

I woke *very* early on Thursday, in the hotel room. I'm not usually very proficient at waking up early, and given a choice I would sleep until noon, unless something exciting's in store for that day!

But the problem was, Mother, Father and myself were all sharing one room. I would never actually *tell* them, of course, as I'm sure they'd be *mortally* wounded from the embarrassment — well, Mother would anyway, Father would just think it funny — but *both* of them were snoring at a *most* terrifying volume. *"A noise fit to wake snoozin' bears in their cave up inside yonder mountain,"* would be how Father might describe such loud snoring.

He DOES talk quite funny, but I like it.

So I simply lay there, becoming more awake with each passing moment, listening to the different rhythms of their snoring — Father's deep slow bear-like growl, Mother's higher, daintier snores almost pretty somehow — until another noise interrupted.

Muffled footsteps, a slight bump, a shuffle of paper — paper pushed under the door and into our room!

Father grunted! I was certain he'd woken — but he simply rolled over, resumed his snoring again, although not quite so loudly.

Whoever was outside scurried quietly, swiftly away then. I heard no door open or close.

There was no doubt they'd pushed something under the door. Quietly, with greatest care I pushed back my blanket, pivoted my legs out of bed, lowered my feet to the floor.

A squeak! Silly sprung bed!

But nobody woke.

I don't really know why I kept so quiet. I suppose, thinking back on it now, I was simply enjoying playing the sleuth — ever since I first read *The Woman in White,* I have longed to go secretly sleuthing, solving the mysteries of intricate murders, apprehending wrongdoers and ... *oh yes, I almost forgot, the note under the door!*

Sneaking stealthily across the floor to the door, I bent down — my knees made a crack so loud it should have woken the sleepers in the *next* room, yet still no one stirred.

Heart pounding, I picked up the sheet of paper.

Should I return to my bed?

What if someone's been kidnapped, and this is the ransom demand, and the person loses their life because I faltered at this moment of greatest import?

I reached for the latch, and ever so silently, slowly, stealthily, unlocked the door.

"Mary?"

"Yes, Father?"

Would he even HEAR me over the great pounding drum of my heartbeat?

"Why you outta bed?"

"I ... I need to use the quincy[1], Father."

"You know you can't go outta this room alone, girl. Wait up a moment." Then he mumbled to himself, "Almost three."

I don't know HOW he knows what time it is, but somehow he always seems to.

I hid the note — *I still don't know why, really* — as Father climbed out of bed and escorted me out of our room and down the hall to the little indoor bathroom.

I went in, locked the door, sat down and *ever-so-quietly* opened the letter.

Newsprint! A mysterious note, laboriously and intricately manufactured from newsprint!

two DAys to leavE CHEYENNE FRakEs oR your faMILy DIe

Well, what would *you* have done? I couldn't very well just tell Father — he's so *very* protective of Mother and I, he'd take us back home to Santa Monica immediately!

And I am *so* looking forward to seeing my old home — not to mention spending more time with Mister Wally, and Mister Deputy Emmett and his lovely family, and dear Mrs Benson, and our lovely new friend Mrs Abbott.

I *will* have to take extra care from now on — and of *course* I'll show Father the note if the nasty person who left it tries anything!

I'm not a complete fool, you know!

But as Father has taught me, most of the things people worry about don't much matter — and besides, I *am* clever enough to work out who left this mean note, if I only apply my mind to it, and give it some time.

So of course, I did what *anyone* would have — I carefully hid away the note, washed my hands in the basin and dried them, unlocked the door and took Father's hand to go back to our room.

"Don't let on to your Mother about how she snores," he said, smiling in the dim light. "She'd faint right away if she knew she snores like a bear. Sure glad I don't snore."

I squeezed his hand and yawned, feigned tiredness by blinking a little — even though I could *not* have been more awake than I was at that exciting moment.

He picked me up, carried me back, *ker-plonked* me down onto my bed, kissed me on the forehead.

Then I lay there the rest of the night, trying to figure out *who* might have left such a note — or rather, I *would* have spent the whole night in that manner, but I fell asleep quite soon after.

It's tiring work, you know, sleuthing. But I'll find the culprit, I will, I promise — or my name isn't Mary Frakes-Farmer-Wilson!

---

1. QUINCY: An indoor toilet

CHAPTER 36
RACE DAY

Raceday dawned perfect and clear, the gray of first light crisp and cool — a promise of a good day to come, as we went about our morning rituals.

By the time the sun itself came to join us, there was clouds all along the horizon, all drifting along like great herds of wild horses — that's how some a'them Indians tell it anyway, and that's what I sometimes see in the shapes when I look at the clouds.

And today, them wild-horse clouds seemed to me like a colorful gift from the Lord up on high — for as the sun broke on through 'em, the colors exploded into the world, warmed our hearts as well as our bodies, with their yellows and purples and oranges, and a flaming red you coulda cooked breakfast on if you coulda got a bit closer.

We stayed out of Wally's way mostly, it being race day he had his own way of preparing, and he needed some space to do things just right.

Every so often he got me or Mary to help him with

something or other, and before too long we was ready to head to the racecourse, good and early, our spirits all high.

I was surprised when he wanted to take the buckboard along, but Wally said it would be easier than carrying everything. "Easier to handle the horses as well. I like to give them some room while we walk to the racecourse, in case of surprises, so no one gets hurt."

He did not saddle the racehorses, and for the first part of the trip we walked them along, slow and quiet, while Georgina and Mary drove along on the buckboard. Ol' Horse weren't too chuffed about being tied to the back a'the buckboard — but he didn't mind once we got going, as he had little Dewdrop for company.

Me and Wally talked a little as we walked along, and it was a most pleasant way to spend a fine morning.

He told me he'd decided to ride both his own horses in their races today — even if he got the chance to give the Cup mount to a good jockey.

"Never understood why you *wouldn't* just ride 'em yourself," I said, walking the gelding around a puddle in the middle of the trail.

"I'm heavier than I look, Lyle. And these races are set weights — meaning, the horses only have to carry a hundred-and-ten pounds. Young John Cartwright could make the weight easy, but I'm almost one-twenty myself, plus the saddle and all — lot of extra weight for a small horse to carry."

"Only ten extra pounds? Ain't much for a fit strong horse is it?"

"Ten pounds *plus* the saddle and blanket. The race is a

mile and a quarter. That extra weight will cost the horse maybe five lengths. We won by three lengths up in Sidney, if you see what I'm saying, Lyle."

"Maybe you *should* hire a jockey."

"I would if I knew one to trust. Too easy for a jockey to make a mistake — *accidental-a-purpose,* my meaning — especially when Lulu here is Cup favorite. Somebody would pay well for a jockey to throw the race, see?"

"Ruin everything, greedy skunks, don't they?"

"They surely do try to," he replied.

After a few minutes silence, I said, "What's all them buckets and boxes and drums in the wagon for anyway?"

"Some are special feed for before the race, some for after. One has a liniment in it, another has somethin' special I made up last night, just in case we might need it to prove something useful."

I tried to read his face for the meaning of what he'd just said, but he only looked at me blankly.

"You'd a'made a fine poker player, Wally."

"Or maybe some sorta chemist," he answered, wiggling his eyebrows a little.

Tells me nothin' at all, but I guess he'll tell me if he needs to.

A half-hour into our walk we stopped in a nice little clearing and all drank some water. It was one a'them pretty little places with a sparkling stream running through it, and just enough trees around to frame the view of the farther-off mountains.

Coulda sat there an hour, just thinkin' and watchin' and

enjoyin' that view — but a'course, we had things needed doing.

I told my girls then that they should stay away from the Abbotts today, it being a race day they'd need their time to themselves.

Georgina was suspicious right off — *reads me like a book* — but Mary said, "Only the handsome young men, do you mean, but not their lovely mother? We *can* talk to Mrs Abbott, can't we, well of course she would be very hurt if we didn't, don't you think?"

"She likely won't be there," I said. "But if she is, we should only talk to her if she's alone. They have two horses running in the Cup, and will have to talk to their owners and such, and their hands will already be full without us taking up all their time."

Georgina narrowed her eyes, stared all the way into me. "Owners? What owners?"

"They train them two horses, not own 'em," I told her. "And their owners will know we're with Wally — they won't like it none if they see the boys talking to us."

"But their horses don't have a chance anyway, Father. When Mother and I were speaking to them after trackwork on Wednesday, a friend of theirs walked by and asked them why they'd even *bothered* entering them into the Cup race. Said they'd gotten even *slower* than they'd been in previous weeks. It was mean, I thought, for it's not like the poor horses can help it — they can't *all* be fast."

"It's true, Kit," said Georgina. "Though they were quite nice-looking horses. Anyway, we'll keep away from the

Abbotts, but if they say hello, well of course we won't run away from them. They seem very nice boys."

Nice boys who kill when they have to? Was the thought crossed my mind.

But I only said, "One thing to *seem* nice, another to *be* it. I said keep away from them boys, and that's what you'll do. Things ain't always how they seem."

Wally had stayed quiet, listening to all a'this, looking at his two horses. He ended our uncomfortable silence by saying, "Time to get going?"

We moved on out again, making our way toward the racecourse at a leisurely pace.

But not two minutes later, as we headed around a bend in a wooded part of the trail, a graveled voice called out from in front of us, in the trees off to one side.

"Touch that gun, Frakes, and I'll fill your damn family with lead. Just give me a reason!"

CHAPTER 37

"JUST SHOOT FRAKES IF HE SO MUCH AS BREATHES. THE MONEY DON'T MATTER!"

When that gravel-voiced feller made his threat, Georgina pulled the buckboard up quick — and there weren't a thing we could do.

And right away, another voice, this one sorta squeaky, came from the opposite side a'the trail, a little behind and left of me.

"Hands up, Frakes. You too, Davis. Just behave and no one gets hurt."

"What the hell do you two fools want?" I growled over my shoulder. I was leading a horse with my left hand, and I lifted my right hand into the air, but not too far from the pocket where my little Remington Rider was.

"They're after all our betting money, Father," said Mary.

Strange thing for the child to say, was my thought. *At least Georgina knows to keep quiet.*

Then as the front feller stepped outta the bushes toward her, Mary added, "Oh, Father, I *told* you to carry half that cash on your person, and not put it *all* in the back of the wagon. Now they'll find the whole thousand dollars!"

"Nice try, little girl," said the road agent skunk. "But we ain't here for your money." He was tall, heavy built, wore all black — including a black bandana tied over his face to hide all his features.

Same feller who beat young John Cartwright, I'd bet plenty on that.

"They've come for my horses," said Wally. "You won't hurt them, will you, you men? I can live with not winning these races, but don't harm my horses, please? I *will* get the horses back, won't I?"

"We'll let you know where to find 'em tonight," said Black Bandana, and his voice sure was overly prideful. "Just don't cause us no problems. We'll tie you up here, and someone'll likely come by before long, let you loose. Main thing, you don't mess with our plans for the races today. If that young fool stablehand done as I asked, you wouldn't be havin' this trouble. You can blame *him* for all this, I reckon."

"Might as well take their money while we're here," said the squeaky-voiced feller behind me. "Not like the boss pays what we're worth for the risks we keep taking." Then he added, "Keep them hands nice and high, both you men, I'll shoot you if'n I have to."

"Forget about money, we're the fellers who bested Lyle damn Frakes," Black Bandana cried to his friend. "Just shoot Frakes if he so much as breathes. The money don't matter!"

Once again, Mary got herself involved. "Why are you here then if you don't want money, you *silly* man? Or is scaring people your *hobby*? Frankly, you'd be better off taking up knitting, or butterfly hunting, or painting nice pictures of horses, that's quite a good one!" She was waving her arms all about, and even stood up as she spoke — she sure did look tiny right then, and I wished she'd just shut her mouth and let me handle things.

"Sit down, little girl," Black Bandana growled, waving his six-gun around — but it was me he kept his eye on, not her. "Take the horses now, Frank, while I cover you. Tie 'em both to the trees there, then come back and tie these fools up. Make one move, Frakes, and you won't make another one, ever."

"That *would* be a pity, Father," said Mary. "I was really looking forward to another long *train trip*. Ah, such lovely memories! You'd better do what the man says, don't you think, so we can do *that* again?"

Oh, Mary, I thought, as the feller behind took the horse away from me. He took Wally's horse too, and began to lead them away. *I hope you know what you're doing, Mary Frakes, and your mother don't get involved.*

"Keep them hands in the air, Frakes and Davis," growled Black Bandana again, ignoring Georgina and Mary completely.

Twenty-five long seconds later — *twenty-five heartbeats* — the squeaky-voiced feller had tied up the horses, and was making his way back toward us. The Black Bandana skunk laughed his fool laugh again and said, "Take the gun from Frakes's pocket first, Frank. Don't worry, I'll fill him with lead if he so much as moves, I got you covered."

And as he said *'covered,'* Mary fired her little Sharps derringer, *once, twice, three times, rat-tat-tat* at that damn Black Bandana, knocking him every which way from a range of five feet. Same moment, I punched the squeaky-voiced feller so hard there was another cracking sound in the middle of the gunfire, which was his jaw breaking.

Wally took off like a gazelle, ran at the Black Bandana skunk where he'd fell to the ground, kicked the Colt from his grasp, yelled, "Don't shoot no more, Mary."

By then I'd hit the squeaky-voiced skunk two more times, and though his eyes was open, he was lying on the ground, almost as still as a dead man — only difference was, he was breathing — funny thing though, he was laying in a pile of horse-dung that one a'them racers had done when we stopped.

I picked up his six-gun by the barrel, raised it up like as if I was gonna pistol-whip him, but he didn't move none at all — them strange open eyes just kept staring off into nothing.

I gave him a pretty good kick in the ribs anyway. *They had threatened my family.*

"Oh my goodness," Georgina cried then. "Are you alright, Mary?"

The child still stood where she'd been all this time on the wagon. "Oh, I'm perfectly *fine* of course, Mother. I was at the *right* end of the gun that was fired, you see?" And she showed Georgina the little twenty-two Sharps, still smoking away in her hand, like as if a child shooting an outlaw was an everyday thing.

"That one killed or what, Wally?" I called to him, checking the squeaky-voiced feller for extra weapons as he started to groan some.

Mary brung her free hand up to cover her mouth, as the shock of what she had done settled heavy upon her. "I *had* to shoot the man, Father, he was going to *hurt* you! I could tell by the way he was showing off to his friend. Oh, he's *not* dead, is he, Mister Wally? I didn't mean to kill him, just to make him not kill *us,* and just to help Father, and to make the men *stop!* Oh, he *can't* be dead, can he? Is he? Oh, no, he *can't* be!"

"It's alright, Mary, he's fine," Wally assured her. One in each shoulder and one in the thigh, you done good." Then he shook the feller some and said, "Done good, didn't she, you filthy horse-stealin' snake? Beat up my stableboy, will you? Try to get at my horses?"

And as the feller in black tried to crawl away from him, Wally Davis kicked him hard in the face — *once, twice and a third time* — then said, "You got one bullet left in that gun ain't you, Mary? How's about handing it to me, and I'll finish him off? Less a'course he decides to tell us who sent him — well, mister? Who was it sent you? One chance to save your own skin."

CHAPTER 38

HE WAS LIMPING LIKE YOUNG
ROY GRIMM ON A BAD DAY

They didn't tell us who sent 'em, a'course. If Georgina and Mary weren't there, I coulda maybe beat it out of 'em — but most likely not.

There's bad men, and there's *real* bad men — and when the second gives up the names a'the first, they might as well just have shot themselves through the head. Whole lot less painful than what *would* get done to 'em, if they told us the names of their bosses.

We couldn't just leave the skunks there — although it *was* rather tempting. But both men needed medical attention, and if we'd left them there we'd be not much better than they were.

Besides which, they needed locking up, and to pay for their crimes, lawful-like.

Mary started shaking while we tied the skunks up, and it took Georgina awhile to calm the poor child. Wally suggested she might need a small shot of brandy — and yes, he had some a'that too, in with his supplies in the back a'the wagon. It was an old-fashioned sorta suggestion for a small child, but it sure did the trick.

You shoulda seen Mary's face when she swallowed that first sip of brandy. She screwed shut her eyes and wrinkled her nose, then she started a furious blinking — then a noise come up outta her throat like it was on fire. But two sips after that she was more-or-less over the shock of shooting a man — and her wits all came back in a hurry.

"I'm never drinking *that* stuff again," she announced. "Never *ever,* as long as I live!" Then smiling hopefully at me — *a touch glassy-eyed too, I noticed* — she said, "But Father, did you like the way I gave you the message, when I mentioned the train? Did you? Tell me you did!"

"A mighty fine secret message, child," I said. "Now didn't I tell you you'd do what was needed when the time come? You done *real* good, Mary. Saved all of us, *and* the horses. But we best get going now, we got races to win."

Both them skunks had enough use of their legs to climb into the back of the wagon, and once they was up there we tied 'em together, just to make things more difficult for ''em. Couldn't have 'em touching Wally's saddles and such, was the point of it.

The squeaky-voiced feller complained — well, I think he did anyway. Hard to tell with that broken jaw I had given the skunk. I offered to set it for him with my *left* fist — "It'll line it back up straight," I told him, pulling the fist back — but he shook his head, his eyes fearful, and I only laughed.

Them fellers was gonna be in trouble from whoever

sent them, not getting the job done *again* — and they'd be serving jail-time soon, once we handed them over.

Still, they *had* accomplished one thing that their bosses would be happy with — Wally Davis was now limping like young Roy Grimm on a bad day.

"What's the problem?" I asked him, when I seen he couldn't hardly put weight on the leg.

"It ain't good, Lyle," he said, as we went to untie his two horses so we could get going. "I don't even know how I did it, or when. So charged up with all the excitement, I never noticed til now, on the way over here. And it's gettin' worse every step."

Looked mighty helpless, he did. This could ruin his chances to win them two races for sure.

"Maybe it'll come right in a minute," I told him. "Sit a spell while I get the horses."

It didn't come right that first couple of minutes. And even though we'd left nice and early, time would soon be our enemy if we didn't keep moving.

I helped Wally onto the box seat to sit with Georgina, while Mary took over his job leading one of the horses.

At one point that Black Bandana feller was causing a problem — point-blank refused to shut up all his moaning.

"Why should I? You can't do nothin' else to me," he said. "That damn little girl shot me to pieces when I wasn't even looking, it just ain't right. I'll moan all I want to."

"That *what* little girl, did you say, skunk?"

"That's worse than calling him old," I heard Wally say, as Georgina pulled on the brake of the wagon, shrugged her shoulders and said, "Just be quick, Kit."

Whenever my wife calls me Kit I know I'm in her good books — and that was all the permission I needed.

I went back there and punched him one right on his jaw. That jaw weren't made of glass like the other feller's was, but what with them two being tied up together he couldn't roll with the punch, and he moaned all the worse then, and spat out some blood with a piece of tooth in it.

"You got five seconds to shut up your moaning, less you want some more."

He moaned again, and I counted to five — same sorta countin' method I'd used quite recent with Little Wayne Logan.

"Five," I said, and hit him again, this time a left hook to his ear. "Can you manage to shut your mouth *now?*"

Skunk closed his eyes, bit down on his tongue and he nodded.

He was quiet from then on.

CHAPTER 39

"AIN'T ARMED NOW, IS SHE...?"

We arrived at the racecourse with time to spare in the end.

Mary and Georgina had been a little regretful that we'd missed the big parade through the streets of Cheyenne yesterday — but they hadn't missed out on it, really.

Thing was, Friday's parade was repeated all over again at the racecourse. Marching bands, tumblers and jugglers, even floats of showgirls all kicking their legs way up high — *I didn't look a'course, but somebody told me it happened* — and as luck had it, we arrived right during the festivities.

Helpful, that was, in a way. We was able to sneak in sort of unnoticed — unnoticed by most anyway — soon as we drove in, Deputy Emmett Slaughter came over to see us.

He was on duty, a'course. Every Deputy in town had been pulling double duty this past two days, in addition to the Federal Marshal Service having men who followed the horse racing carnivals around to keep things above board.

Emmett told me he hadn't learned nothing important yet, and I told him he'd best go get one a'them Federal Deputies to arrest two bad skunks we had in the back of our wagon.

He took a quick look and said, "Is the one all in black the man who tried to kill young John Cartwright?"

"Admitted as much," I said.

That sure got that feller's beady eyes opened up wide, as he sat there still bleeding and battered.

"So, attempted murder of Cartwright," said Emmett. "Plus four more instances of the same charge today? For both of them this time, of course."

"Splits fair I reckon," I told him. "Although maybe one of 'em might start thinkin' clear, give us the name of his boss, save himself from the charges?"

"I know I would," said Emmett. "Whichever one talks first will get the lenient treatment. Well, I'll go fetch the Federal Deputies now, unless one of you men wish to talk."

"Don't do it, Frank," growled Black Bandana. But by the way Squeaky-Voice Frank's busted jaw was all swelled, he could not have talked anyway.

He just looked at Emmett, the fear strong in his eyes, and briefly shook his head, *No.*

As Emmett went to fetch the Federal Deputies, me and Georgina and Mary had work to do.

Wally still couldn't walk, so Mary went to find him a stick to use for a crutch, while Georgina and me done everything Wally told us.

Young Roy Grimm came over to give us a hand, and a good thing he did. With Wally more-or-less crippled for the moment, we needed a man who was used to handling horses on race day — and while Roy only did so a half-dozen race days each year, he knew all the right things to do.

It took fifteen minutes of fetching and carrying, but in the end, the horses was all settled in to their stables to rest up before their races.

Once Roy was done helping Wally, he went off to help someone else — but not before promising he'd be back to handle both horses when it came time to saddle them up and be led out to the track for their races.

One a'them Federal Deputies came and took our statements a bit after that. We told him the truth of what happened, but didn't say nothing yet about who we believed they might be working for. Last thing we needed was for the Mayor and the Sheriff to know we was just about onto 'em.

The two traveling Federal Deputies was brothers, as it turned out. One seemed surprised little Mary had fired the shots that had saved us — but the other pointed out how dangerous their own older sister had been as a child, which caused the first one to nod his head in agreement.

"Ain't armed now, is she?" he said, watching Mary stroke the neck of a horse. "It being illegal to carry a firearm of *any* sort, here at the racecourse on race day."

I looked that Federal Deputy right in the eye and said, "You think I'm so foolish as to let her carry a gun *here,* with all these people around? It's locked away, just like it should be."

"Just checking, sir," he replied.

What he don't know won't hurt him. And the child's well trained.

The Deputies told us this weren't the first time they've locked someone up for attempting to stop a horse getting to the racecourse. Best thing was, they have their own wagon they travel with — a little portable office and jail-cell — so if it *was* the Mayor and the Sheriff who sent Black Bandana and Squeaky-Voice Frank, they would not find out for awhile. At least not til tonight anyway, when the Marshals would deliver the men to the County hoosegow — my main meaning being, they wouldn't find out unless these Federal men were crooks too. And that seemed unlikely.

Soon as both horses was all settled into their race day stalls, Wally got to work massaging a most evil-smelling horse liniment into his leg. "If it comes even half-right, I'll be able to ride," he said hopefully.

"If the smell a'that liniment don't kill you first," I replied, and walked around upwind of him. "Nine Oils, is it?"

"My own brew of it, much better," he said. "Heavy on camphor, light on the brick oil, and enough oil of vitriol in it to wake up a dead man."

"And kill him all over again as soon as he wakes!" I took another step backways, pinching my nose shut to keep out the sulfurous stink of it.

The stables at the Cheyenne track have a view of the racecourse, and pretty soon after we got settled in, the horses went out on the track for the opening race.

It's been years since I've been at a horserace, and I'd almost forgotten how exciting the racing can be.

Wally reckoned the number ten horse had been pretty unlucky in Sidney last week. Finished third in a harder event, after missing the start and running on strong at the finish in a bit shorter race. I made a small wager, and a good thing I *did* keep it small — seems like unluckiness follows some animals around, just the same as some people.

Number ten got squeezed back at the start, got boxed in as they went along the back straight, then had to go six horses wide the whole way round the bend. *'Rattled home the last furlong'* — Mary's words, those — and got beaten by a half-length.

Wally nodded a wise one as he sat there guarding his horses, on a chair that Mary had found him to rest on.

"Guess they should not a'named that horse Lucky Jim," I said as I tore up my betting slip. "It's a jinx when you name someone *Lucky,* in my opinion."

"Or maybe they shoulda trained him to jump nice and straight at the start," Wally said. "Instead of jumping in the air how he did, is all I mean, Lyle. He did that same thing last week in Sidney you know — that's why I didn't bet on him today."

"Thanks for the tip, old friend," I said, shaking my head. "Maybe next time, you'll tell me the whole thing *before* I go throw my money down the outhouse."

For a man with a painful sore leg, Wally sure did look mighty amused.

CHAPTER 40
THE DARK HORSE

With eight races scheduled for the day, I decided I'd learned my lesson on betting — I'd wait for Wally's horses to run, put my money on them.

Least I knew they was properly trained.

Wally's horses were in race four and race eight — the last race of the day was the Cup race, a'course.

Only thing about that was, the bookmakers would take bets on the big Cup race all day.

When I'd looked at the betting markets before the first race, Wally's horse was the even-money favorite — *one-to-one, another way to say it* — each dollar you bet you'd win a dollar, plus get your own dollar back too, a'course.

"Not hardly worth it," I heard someone say, but when his friend pointed out he would double his money in a race of just over two minutes, he agreed it made *much* more sense than betting on a loser at long odds.

Other thing I noticed then, was the betting odds on the

Abbott-trained horses. Their gelding — his name was Crying Tiger — started the day at odds of fifteen-to-one. But their mare, The Dark Horse, was even less respected, completely unwanted it seemed, at twenty-to-one.

When I went back to the stalls and told Wally about it, he didn't seem worried at all. He just said, "Don't bet til later, we'll get better odds."

A steady stream of people came by — some he knew, some he didn't — all trying to look at his horses. But no one could really see into the stalls from behind the rope that the public weren't allowed past.

Sometimes these folk asked Wally questions, and he answered different people in different ways. Seemed like they was all trying to get a little inside information. My old friend occasionally hobbled across to the rope to whisper things to them — then they'd smile like cats that seen cream, and scurry away.

During one such occasion, I did hear one feller say, "No! You can't be serious, Mister Davis! Surely you can't ride the horse today in *your* condition."

And young Wally just answered, "I'd best go sit down, get some more a'that liniment into it — I might yet come good, and what else can I do?"

It all seemed pretty mysterious, even to me. But I knew he weren't faking. No one woulda put that stinkin' stuff on without a real good reason.

"Nothing like adding some fuel to the fire on a racecourse," Wally told me soon after, looking plenty relaxed.

Mary and Georgina had been wandering about,

enjoying the various stalls and little shows here and there. There was even a feller who could swallow a sword, Mary told me when they returned. She begged me to accompany her to his tent, where we would see the trick done, at a cost of just ten cents apiece.

Georgina could not stand the thought of it, let alone bring herself to watch, so it was left up to me to go with the child.

"Check the Cup odds again while you're there," Wally said as Mary and me started walking away. "They'll change through the day as folks start to bet, and it might be of interest — in more ways than one."

Mary didn't know what that final bit meant, but I surely did — if the Mayor and the Abbotts really did have a ring-in, the bets would start before long, and the betting odds would change.

But for now, it was time for my little girl to enjoy all the fun of the fair.

"Look, Father," she said as we came close to the tent. "He calls himself *The Superb Samuel Swallow, Performer of Outrageous & Impossible Feats!*"

"Don't guess you need to change *his* name?" I said.

"We'll see how good he is first," Mary answered, gripping my hand as I took out two dollars to pay our way into the tent. "If he disappoints us, I'll change it to *Silly Sam Swallow, Sinful Swiper of Cents.*"

"Dang dollar drainer, more like," I replied, as we went in and sat to one side near the corner, where I could see everyone.

Not only did the sword-swallower do the trick just as

advertised, he also appeared to drink boiling oil, followed up by molten lead — all this without getting so much as a speck of dust on his bright fancy clothing. Then he blew fire out of his mouth, causing one woman in the front row to faint right away — thereby ending the show as the performer came to her aid.

I knew none of it was real, but it *seemed* like it, and that was the main thing. *Quite a showman,* I thought, observing the wonder on my little Mary's face when the flashy-dressed feller revived the fainted woman, simply by sprinkling her face with some invisible substance.

For a child who's been through so much, her capacity for joy never ceases to astound me.

A dollar each had seemed steep at first — but I'd have paid a hundred to see Mary smile that smile.

We went then and checked on the odds as Wally requested, and something of interest *had* happened.

Crying Tiger had gone out to twenty-to-one odds now, but The Dark Horse was now ten-to-one, and folks nearby were whispering her name, as the odds tumbled further while I was watching. We stood there until the second race started — there was forty-five minutes between every race — and by then, the Abbott mare's odds were down to seven-to-one.

We watched the horses thunder down the straight in race two, which Mary enjoyed even better than I did, I reckon. Shakes the whole ground under your feet it does, a large field of horses galloping hard all at once — it's quite an experience. Then we walked back to the stables where Wally was waiting for news.

"Lose again, Lyle?" he asked with a twinkle in his eye.

"No, I won this time — by not betting."

"Best way to win, that," he said, winking at Mary. "Any change in the odds?"

"Your lovely Light of My Life is still even money," Mary told him with excitement. "But the rumor mill is all for The Dark Horse — *she's* well supported at seven-to-one and attracting a veritable *slew* of admirers."

"Well," young Wally Davis replied, "I got no idea what a *vestibule stew* is, but the drop to seven-to-one odds means some pretty big money's been invested. Best you get down there and follow anyone who's betting big money on her, Lyle, and see who they deliver their tickets to."

"No problem, but where's my good wife gone?"

"I sent her to find me a jockey," he said, sounding heavy of heart. "This leg ain't gonna come good to ride Wild West Willie in race four, so I'll just have to risk it. And with Willie being the favorite, I'll learn if the jock can be trusted to ride in the Cup, in case my leg's still no good. He rides five pounds over the weight, but his racing skill more than makes up for it."

This time I left Mary with Wally — she wanted to help me with my sleuthing job, but Wally persuaded her to stay, telling her she needed to keep watch on the horses while he hobbled to the outhouse using the stick we had found him.

By the time I got back to the betting ring, the place was abuzz with all sorts of rumors. Word was that Wally's Cup horse might be injured, as there had been an incident on its way to the track. I heard one feller whisper to another that Light of My Life had run off when shots had been fired, which was why she'd arrived at the track somewhat late.

Well, there was a *seed* of truth in all that — and I sure had to wonder who'd started the rumor, and why.

It had also come out that the regular jockey, John Cartwright, was lying in hospital battered and bruised — some folks even believed he was dead! And that Wally Davis would ride Light of My Life himself, fourteen pounds over her allotted weight! *And* that Wally could not walk!

Again, some truth mixed with scuttlebutt, but where had it come from?

But the betting, it sure told a story. Light of My Life was now two-to-one odds, and it seemed like everyone wanted to bet on The Dark Horse.

Wally WANTED them rumors to all get around, to improve the odds on his own horse!

As I watched, a little man darted toward the last bookmaker still giving four-to-one odds for The Dark Horse. That dapper little feller looked just how a rat would — if you dressed it up in a stripey brown suit and a small bowler hat — and he wore highly polished leather shoes that squeaked every step.

"Five-hundred on The Dark Horse," he said, in a voice so high and squeaky it drowned out the noise of his shoes.

"Two-thousand to five-hundred The Dark Horse," the bookmaker's mouthpiece shouted as he took the money. "That's it, the odds are now two-to-one." Then he called, "I'll give three-to-one Light of My Life, if anyone wants it. Light of My Life at threes!"

I was just about tempted to bet, but I stuck to my task, and followed the rat-lookin' feller through the crowd at a distance.

He was easy to follow alright — the damn squeak his shoes made coulda been heard by dogs down in Denver, and set 'em to howling.

I stood behind a pole at the corner of the grandstand, watched him walk up into it, all the way to the top — and who should be there to greet him but Mayor Reginald Fisk. The skunk Mayor was all dressed up in a fancy evening suit, and waving a cane around in the air, of all things, as he laughed it up with a drink in his other hand.

"Tell the world now," he shouted, raising the drink in the air as if making a toast. Then his voice boomed out all around as he cried, "The Mayor of Cheyenne gives his townsfolk the winner of their Cup race. A gift from your Mayor to his citizens! Bet up, all you voters, get down there and lay down your money! The Dark Horse will *not* be beaten, you can trust me on that! You may thank me with your support, next month on Voting Day."

CHAPTER 41

WILD WEST WILLIE

I made for the stalls to tell Wally right away — but as I walked by the betting ring it made for quite a sight, so I stopped a few moments to watch. Men was actually *fighting* each other to be first to bet on The Dark Horse!

"Three-hundred to two-hundred The Dark Horse," I heard one bookmaker cry. "Now even money!"

And another called out, "I'll give four-to-one Light of My Life — *someone* must want her!"

When I told Wally all that I'd seen, he quietly said, "I'd give a thousand dollars to see into that stable their mare's in right now. They know mine's a pretty fair horse — still, it *couldn't* be Jessy Gillespie. It *couldn't.*"

By the time young Roy Grimm led Wild West Willie into the parade yard, so the jockey could mount up for race four, the whole crowd was giddy with excitement and anticipation.

Some folks had already bet all their money on The

Dark Horse for the last race — but many held back, trying instead to build up a bank on the other races beforehand.

But the one thing they *all* seemed to agree on, was that the Mayor's horse could not be beaten in the big Cup race. She would win *"in a romp."*

We watched Wally's gelding go out onto the track — he was quite some horse, Wild West Willie. He looked big, fit and strong, his coat gleaming under the sunlight. The jockey Wally had hired had been a professional down in Kentucky for several years, before his ballooning weight had cost him too many rides, and he'd joined the *'traveling race circus'* only a year ago.

Wild West Willie was an even money favorite, and Wally said that was good odds. He stayed with his Cup horse to guard her a'course, and gave me and Georgina his betting money to wager.

"Don't put the bets on if any really big money comes for another horse," he told us. "If they offer two-to-one about Willie, I'll know the jockey's crooked."

But he need not have worried at all — the horse stayed a solid even money bet the whole time, and when the horses arrived at the starting area we bet the money Wally had given us — plus quite some of our own.

As I watched through my spyglass, Wild West Willie jumped straight to the lead at the start — but soon after, the jockey allowed two other horses to go by him, and went along quietly in third place for most of the race, going easy with his head on his chest.

But soon as they turned into the stretch — *"Two furlongs to go,"* Mary called, *"Go, Willie, go!"* — the jockey asked the horse for an effort. He raced to the lead as they passed the furlong marker, and ran away with the win by two lengths, barely raising a sweat.

Young Roy Grimm was sure happy too — Wally had been sure to tell the young feller to bet, as he'd definitely fixed up the fetlock.

And the best thing of all? *Wally now knew he could trust the jockey to ride Light of My Life in the Cup race.*

Young Roy held onto the horse while the jockey and saddle got weighed — they do it after each race out in front of the crowd, so as folks can be certain the horse carried the weight he was meant to. They put weights made of lead in pockets sewed into the saddle, if the jockey's too light. It's a tense moment, waiting for the jockey to weigh in — every so often, they lose a piece of lead from the saddle, in which case the horse gets disqualified.

No problems for this race, all three place-getters weighing in fine. The Steward gave the All Clear, allowing the bookmakers to pay out the bets, the race result now all official.

"That there couple of minutes is where those engaged in a ring-in might still be nervous," Wally explained as I showed him all our betting tickets. "Result ain't official til then. Thing is, at this point we can be pretty certain the Mayor's horse is a ring-in. But because we have a murder to prove, I can't do what I'd like to, this situation."

I nodded, put the tickets away in my pocket. "So we have to let the horse run, not say a word?"

"That's the size and shape of it, Lyle. And *maybe,* their mare will be faster than mine. But I got a trick up my sleeve anyway — so after race six, bring Roy Grimm up here, and young Emmett Slaughter too, if you can. I got a bit of a plan. If we do the thing right, we just might be able to catch them all out on the ring-in."

"And from there, facing long jail-time, the Abbotts *might* tell the truth, and give up the Mayor as being the killer."

"That's what I'm hoping," said Wally.

Mary and Georgina had watched the race from down by the finish line, and gone to stand nearby while Roy washed the winning horse down and watered him proper.

The three of them now walked toward us, triumphant and happy — *four of 'em if you count the horse* — but before they came within earshot Wally said, "Not a word to the ladies, we'll need to keep them away later on for their safety, in case it goes badly."

A minute or two of thanks and congratulations followed, and Wally made a fuss of Willie and fed him lumps of sugar. Then Mary held up her hand and said, "Did you hear *that,* Father? Everyone, shhhh."

We all listened up, and the race-announcer feller on the speaking-trumpet was jawing on about some sorta shootin' competition, which was about to be held right on the racecourse, out front a'the grandstand.

"Neat trick," I said, "havin' a shootin' contest when there's no guns allowed in the place."

"They supply them," said Mary. "Can we both...? *Oh,* that just isn't fair — you must be *sixteen* years or over to enter."

"Go enter your *mother* in the contest," I told her.

Georgina's head spun toward me and her eyes flashed a warning. But even she seen the funny side after a second.

"I'd best not enter," she said. "Might *accidentally* shoot my own husband."

"I'm sure he'd be perfectly safe if you *aimed* at him, Mother," Mary said with a laugh, and Georgina laughed too. "Oh, please, Father, you *must* try to win it. There's a hundred dollar prize, and I'm certain you'll win, and ... *please?*"

"I'll give it a go then," I told her. "Hundred extra to bet on the winner a'the Cup might be handy, now she's four-to-one odds."

CHAPTER 42
THE CHEYENNE SHOOTING CONTEST

When I walked through the open gate onto the racetrack, it struck me right away how half a'the shootin' contest entrants was drunk.

The whiskey had flowed mighty freely in the carnival atmosphere, and what with it being more than halfway through the day, there was more glassy eyes and red noses than ordinary ones.

Even Sheriff Cal Pettygore looked like he'd partook of a couple too many — and the way he mouthed off at me proved it.

"What are you out here for, Frakes?" he said with a chuckle. "Too old to see small targets, ain't you? You been seen around town with eyeglasses on, so I hear."

I made a great show of squinting at the fool and said, "Who *is* that? Come a bit closer so I can see." Then I sniffed at the air there between us and said, "Oh, it's Sheriff Cal Pettygore, a'course. Only skunk I ever met that smells worse than a real actual skunk. You sure you ain't too drunk to shoot straight, young Sheriff? Won't be a good look when you lose to an old man like me."

He was twenty years younger than myself — and twenty years easier to bait.

"Wouldn't care to make a wager on the outcome, Frakes, would you? I know you're cashed up, as I seen you bet on your friend's horse that just won race four. And I got fifty dollars to say you can't beat me in this contest. Or are you afraid?"

"How 'bout we make it a hundred, young Cal?"

"Hundred it is, Frakes, you're on."

There was three tables set up on the lush racecourse grass. One a'them tables was covered in all sorts a'guns, but the other tables captured my interest soon as I seen 'em. The second had a huge spyglass sitting on it pointed down the home straight a'the racetrack — biggest spyglass I ever saw — but the final table won the contest for grabbing my interest. It was covered with a huge great contraption that looked like a cross between a voice-trumpet, an elephant, and a set of Scotch bagpipes.

So this was the *'marvel of modern engineering,'* Mary had been begging me to go see. Well, she sure weren't wrong when she said it was worth a close look.

Musta took a half-dozen men to carry it down here — not to mention the cost a'the brass they had made the thing from.

The contest judge had us stand in a line, and the racecourse announcer stepped up to his voice-trumpet bagpipes elephant-lookin' invention, and told us — and the spectators too — what the rules were.

Well, I'll tell you one thing, I sure weren't prepared for the noise that thing made from close up. My dang ears near jumped off of my head and went lookin' for water when he talked in his end a'the monstrosity.

"WELCOME TO THE CHEYENNE RACE CLUB SHOOTING CONTEST," he began.

Well, the dang noise was too much for the nervy feller standin' next to me — he jumped back a step, then ran on the spot while waving his arms all about, like as if he was under attack by a swarm of crankified bees!

"Best stand back a picayune from it," I said. "You near busted this poor feller's eardrums."

The announcer smiled a weak one, adjusted his stance and went on — still *real* loud, but not so bad it damaged our ears.

"THE JUDGE'S DECISION ON ALL MATTERS WILL BE FINAL — PRESIDING OVER THE CONTEST, PLEASE WELCOME THE HONORABLE JUDGE WILCOTT, OUR OWN HEAD MAGISTRATE AND PRESIDENT OF CHEYENNE RACE CLUB."

There was respectful applause, the besuited, neat-bearded Judge held up his hand for the crowd to stop, and we got to the rules.

"FIRST ROUND WILL BE WITH RIFLES, SECOND ROUND PISTOLS, THEN CONTINUE TO ALTERNATE — TARGET IS A STANDARD PLAYING CARD STUCK TO A BOARD — DISTANCE TO INCREASE EVERY ROUND — ANY MAN WHO MISSES THE TARGET IS OUT OF THE CONTEST — CONTESTANTS MAY CHOOSE ANY WEAPON

FROM THE WIDE SELECTION ON THE TABLE — ALL GUNS ARE SUPPLIED AND LOADED BY KELVIN MOORE OF MOORE'S GUN EMPORIUM, CHEYENNE, AND ARE GUARANTEED TO SHOOT STRAIGHT — A BIG THANK YOU TO KELVIN, HOW ABOUT IT, FOLKS?"

Once again there was cheers from the crowd, and we got down to business.

First two fellers missed the whole board completely, let alone got near the playing card. Dang board, so-called, was a table set up on its end. I reckon Horse coulda hit it if I let him use Gertrude.

Sheriff Cal Pettygore was next up — even with a few drinks under his belt, he weren't likely to miss with a rifle at seventy-five yards.

The Judge looked through his big fancy spyglass, then spoke to the announcer.

"PUT YOUR HANDS TOGETHER FOR OUR VALIANT SHERIFF," the announcement boomed out to the crowd. "SHERIFF CAL PETTYGORE, FIRST MAN THROUGH TO ROUND TWO!"

I was up next, hit the card an inch left of center with the nice Henry rifle I'd chose. *This gun'll do me,* I decided. *Now on, I'll aim a smidge to the right.*

Of the twenty-five men who had entered, most chose one or another of the Winchesters, but surprisingly few hit the target — mostly due to the whiskey, I guess, but also, by the end a'the round a crosswind had sprung up, and it made things tricky.

Next round was with six-guns, and the Sheriff was first

man to shoot. Used his own Colt, I noticed, which weren't allowed by the rules, but I didn't care.

Whatever gun Pettygore used, he'd be there at the end unless somethin' strange happened. First time me and him ever met was during a shooting contest some years back — he had took his loss that day ungraciously, and I'd never liked the man since. But the truth was, I only beat him in the last round on account of good luck more than anything else.

Not much of a man, but a mighty capable shootist, Calvin J Pettygore.

CHAPTER 43
WHAT THE KID HAD BEEN HIDING

First revolver I picked up was a nice Smith & Wesson — felt perfectly balanced in the hand, and Kel smiled a little and said, "Good gun, that, Lyle."

I trusted the man, and he'd done good work for me before, converting various weapons over the years, so I wasted no extra time, said, "Best load it up then."

He placed a single bullet in the chamber, and I stepped up to the line, waited for the wind to die down then squeezed the trigger.

"LYLE FRAKES THROUGH TO ROUND THREE," boomed the verdict out to the folks all assembled to watch.

"I'll buy that six-gun, Kel," I told him with a nod as I handed it back. "When the contest is over, a'course."

With a grin he replied, "Thought you might," as the next man stepped up to the line.

That man rushed his shot, fired as the wind gusted, and missed the card by an inch. "No way I missed," the man growled. "I demand to see the damn target myself, I ain't gonna be cheated by you locals, I'm a dead shot."

"You'll be a dead *man,* from rotting in jail," I warned him, "if you question Judge Wilcott. I'd shut pan[1] if I was you."

"I *will* sight the target myself," he growled, even louder this time. "I ain't trustin' no high-falutin' judge, no matter—"

"Do you *dare* to challenge my integrity?" Judge Wilcott said — not loud, but with absolute authority.

"I just ... that is, no, sir, I just can't see the target from here and—"

"Come look through the telescope," the Judge told him. Then after the feller looked through it, Wilcott poked him hard in the middle of his forehead and said, "Make certain *never* to step out of line, sir. For if *ever* you come before my court, I *shall* remember you. You just *wasted* the one morsel of lenience I allot to each man. Now, begone from my sight."

"Tried to warn you," I said to the fool as he scurried away. Then I nodded a respectful one at the Judge, and he sagely nodded back.

By the time they shifted the targets and we got through another round of rifles and pistols, there was only three of us left.

Me and Cal Pettygore, as I expected — and also, a skinny young kid, a left-hander, who I'd noticed kept hiding behind other men when he could. His hat was worn low and he kept his head down — seemed like he looked at the ground just about the whole time. Other thing strange, he kept his hands in his coat pockets, though it weren't at all cold — only took his *right* hand out to pick up a weapon, and the left hand only made an appearance once he was up at the line, and preparing to shoot.

Curious, that. I'll watch him closer, now on.

The wind had gotten wilder this fifteen minutes we'd been here. Wouldn't be no easy thing to hit a small playing card with a rifle — not now, at a hundred-fifty yards in the tricky conditions.

Problem was, it was such a wide open space that the wind picked up strong, but then it got diverted by the grandstand, the stables, the fences, and all manner of things. Dang wind came from fifteen directions, it seemed to me sometimes.

Pettygore walked to the mark, the wind stopped like as if he was blessed, and he fired the Winchester.

"FIRST MAN THROUGH TO ROUND SIX," the voice boomed. **"OUR OWN CROWD FAVORITE, THE SHERIFF OF CHEYENNE, CAL PETTYGORE!"**

I wasted no time, took advantage of the lull in the breeze, fired my own shot without delay.

"LYLE FRAKES, THROUGH TO ROUND SIX!"

This time I watched the kid close. And you coulda blowed me down with a feather when he took his left hand from his pocket and took a full hold of the Winchester.

That's when I seen what that kid had been hiding.

And I realized then, it was *me* he'd been hiding it from — his left thumb was covered with a bandage, and was maybe about an inch shorter than it shoulda been if the whole thing was there.

Young Bert Harris, age maybe-sixteen, was a recently retired outlaw — a member of the one-time train robbers, known as *The Friend Gang*.

———————————————

1. SHUT PAN: Shut your mouth or Shut up. To use it in an oft-heard sentence, "You're wrong again, JV, and you'd best shut pan if you expect dinner tonight."

CHAPTER 44

"IF HE OPENS HIS BIG MOUTH
AGAIN, I'LL FILL IT WITH FIST..."

"**H**USH PLEASE, EVERYBODY,**"** came the announcement. **"TIME FOR THE SIXTEEN-YEAR-OLD BERT HARRIS TO SHOOT NOW."**

The kid took an age to get ready, shuffling about on his feet, and he seemed awful nervous. The wind was back again, and it would not seem to let up. He would have to shoot soon.

Then right when the kid let his breath halfway out, making ready to shoot, the damn Sheriff Cal Pettygore yelled, "Hurry up, kid, we ain't got all day!"

Lucky for the young feller, he *didn't* squeeze the trigger. He stayed his hand, lifted his head, sucked in a big breath — but did not look around.

Judge scowled but said nothin', a'course — there was no solid rule, but no fair man woulda balked the kid in that way.

"You're a cheatin' skunk, Pettygore," I said. Then I

turned and called, "Take your time, kid, there ain't no hurry. If he opens his big mouth again, I'll fill it with fist."

"I'm the damn *law* here, Frakes," the skunk Sheriff growled. "You can't speak to *me* in that manner!"

I said no more words, took just one step toward him, stood and stared at the filthy damn cheat. What I *wanted* was for him to hit me, and I reckon my eyes told him so.

But after a couple of seconds he looked away, turned about, muttered something I couldn't hear — then he stayed away from us while the young feller gathered his wits and took his shot.

The Judge smiled and nodded at the kid, then spoke into the ear of the announcer.

"RIGHT THROUGH THE CENTER OF THE ACE OF SPADES," boomed the voice, and the crowd applauded the kid. **"BERT HARRIS, EVERYBODY!"**

When the kid brung his Winchester back to the table, I looked into his eyes and said, "Nice shooting ... *FRIEND.* Hope that thumb's healing well."

Well, his eyes went wide with alarm when I said the word *"FRIEND"* — just as I suspected they might. And when I mentioned the thumb his gaze went from me toward the Sheriff, and the youngster looked mightily panicked.

But I only winked at him and said, "Hope you been stayin' outta trouble, son. Don't worry about that damn cheat, you just shoot your best, keep your eyes on that prize."

"Yessir, Mister Frakes," he said with a nod. "Unless you'd rather I—?"

"I'd *rather* you be a man of honor, son. I'll *forgive* what you just suggested, you bein' young and not knowin' no better. But if you miss this time, I *ain't* gonna be happy. You do your best," I said with a nod. "You and me, we got honor, am I right?"

"Yessir, Mister Frakes," said the kid, nodding back. "Yessir, we surely have."

At sixty-five yards, in that wide open place, I figured I could still hit the card with that fine little six-gun. But the wind would have its own ideas of what could and couldn't happen — I surely knew that much.

But when Sheriff Cal Pettygore walked on up to toe the line, and drew out his Colt from his holster, the wind died right away for a moment. He raised up the gun to take aim — and I called, "Wait up a minute there, Sheriff, I got a question for the judge."

Pettygore ignored me at first, and it seemed he would take his shot anyway. But a sudden gust of wind came across, and he turned toward me, his face red and angry.

"What's the meaning of this? You cost me my chance at a shot when the wind wasn't there."

"Hold your horses, young Sheriff," I said. "Is there *really* a wind today? I hadn't noticed." Then I turned to Judge Wilcott and told him, "Pettygore forgot to choose a gun from the table. Rules we got told said he had to — my guess is he musta forgot this one time. I mean, if he used his own gun already, he'd be disqualified, wouldn't he, Judge?"

The rage showed so clear on Sheriff Cal Pettygore's

face then, I thought he might shoot me. "My gun's no better than those on the table. Right, Kelvin?"

"Maybe not even *as* good," Kel Moore replied. "But rules is rules for a reason, right, Judge?"

The judge knew what had been going on, just as well as the rest of us. With the barest hint of a smile he said, "It's lucky you didn't take the shot, Sheriff Pettygore, I'd have had to disqualify you from the contest. You should probably thank Mister Frakes, speaking up when he did. Please choose a weapon now, Sheriff."

"Damn you, Frakes," said Cal — but he holstered his own Colt and moved to the table to pick out one of Kel Moore's.

"I recommend this Smith & Wesson," I told him with a smile, picking it up and offering it to him butt first. "Mighty fine weapon."

He ignored me, chose an Army Colt, same as his own.

Kel Moore loaded it for him, and Pettygore walked to the line. He waited what seemed an age. Finally the wind died, and he took his shot.

Judge looked from his telescope to me, raised his eyebrows, half-smiled then spoke to the announcer beside him.

"OH, THAT'S A SHAME," the announcer boomed out. **"MISSED BY UNDER TWO INCHES — STILL, IT'S NOT OVER YET, FOLKS — IF THE OTHER TWO MEN MISS THE TARGET, THERE WILL BE ONE MORE ROUND WITH THE RIFLES — AND WE KNOW HOW GOOD OUR FINE SHERIFF IS WITH A WINCHESTER!"**

Kel loaded the six-gun — a single bullet, a'course — and I stepped up to the line. I waited for the pesky dang wind to drop, then it did. And just as I squeezed the trigger — *or rather, a tenth-second beforehand* — that damn filthy Pettygore sneezed fit to blow his whole face apart.

"Damn cheat," I said under my breath, soon as the bullet left the chamber.

Announcer didn't need to be told I had missed, we all seen the racecourse fence splinter, a good six feet left of the target.

"WHAT A SHAME," came the great booming voice, as I spun about, walked straight at the cheatin' damn Sheriff, placing the gun on the table as I walked by it.

"Sorry, Frakes," he said, smug as ever you like. "Must be all them fancy flowers that grow by the track here. I'm allergic you know."

"You'll be sneezing out your rear end in a minute then, Pettygore," I growled. "Because I'm gonna uproot that rose bush over there, and shove it so far up your—"

"Gentlemen, please," hissed the Judge. "What was done was unsportsmanlike, and I'm frankly *disgusted* — but there's not a thing I can do, the way the rules stand. As you *clearly* have a problem with each other, please take it elsewhere, not here. Our racing club has its reputation to uphold."

I took another step toward the Sheriff, and said, "What's wrong, Cal? Scared of an old man? You're twenty years younger than me, and still need to hide behind your position as Sheriff. In the old days, men used to be men, settle differences with honor, using their fists."

I think the Judge spoke again, but we was past listening.

"I can't be bothered with an old fart like you, Frakes," Cal Pettygore said — *but he couldn't hold my gaze when he said it.* "You best not be thinking of staying in Cheyenne though. Things might get *uncomfortable* for you, if you know what I mean."

I have never been the sort to hit another man below the belt, so to speak — but I *knew*, really *knew* in my bones, that this skunk had murdered Delvene Abbott's son in cold blood, and it riled me now.

I leaned in toward him, and, striking as low a blow as I ever have, I whispered, "You should probably speak to your Deputies, Cal. They been laughing it up in saloons when they speak of your wife, and what she gets up to when you're on shift."

He stiffened a little, his eyes blazed, and his hand hovered over his holster.

I smiled, said, "I'm unarmed, Cal, remember? Murder would look bad, all a'these folks here watching, and the Mayor wouldn't like it."

His hands made two fists then, as the judge once again said, "Please, gentlemen" — and somewhere in the background the announcer said something about young Bert Harris, stepping up to take his shot.

"Speakin' of your friend the Mayor," I said quietly to Cal, "he's *sure* been enjoying himself — word is your wife prefers him to you, on account of his *size.*"

"He's *half* my damn size," cried the Sheriff as he threw a wild right-hand punch, which I easily blocked.

"Not the bit that matters to her," I laughed, ducking under his left hand, then driving a vicious right fist up into his ribs.

Pettygore wheezed as he doubled over a little, and tried to protect his face with an elbow, as I got all my weight behind a flying left hook — well, his instincts were good, he certainly knew which punch was coming his way — but he was too slow, far too slow.

My left fist crashed into his jaw, and his face was whipped sideways by the impact — a sheet of blood flew from his mouth, and he lost his balance, toppling over onto the lush grass of the Cheyenne home straight.

For a moment, as the Sheriff looked up at me, his eyes mad with hatred, I thought he might go for his gun.

But I extended my hand to the skunk, said, "Reckon we both had enough, Cal. How about you? We should maybe learn to behave out in public, us two."

As he looked at my face then my hand, and considered the offer, we heard the announcement.

"WHAT WONDERFUL SHOOTING, FOLKS, HOW ABOUT THAT — YOUNG BERT HARRIS WINS THE CONTEST —

SIXTEEN YEARS OLD, WHAT A SHOOTIST — LET'S GIVE HIM A HAND!"

"We best acknowledge the young feller's shooting, Cal," I said. "Wouldn't wish to seem like poor losers." My hand was still extended, waiting for him to make up his mind.

Pettygore finally took hold of my hand, I pulled the skunk to his feet, then we stood there applauding young Bert.

Then when the clapping and cheering died down, the announcer — louder than ever — called out, **"PLEASE THANK OUR OWN SHERIFF CAL PETTYGORE AND HIS FRIEND LYLE FRAKES FOR THEIR *VERY* REALISTIC EXHIBITION OF HEAVYWEIGHT BOXING — PUT YOUR HANDS TOGETHER, FOLKS, FOR TWO TOUGH MEN OF THE WEST!"**

"Shake hands you deplorable men," said Judge Wilcott quietly — and as we did so, we got cheered just as loud as young Bert did for all his fine shooting.

As we stood there, two men with hands joined in that moment, Cal Pettygore asked me a question. "Did my wife *really* say she liked *him* because his was bigger?"

No option but to tell him the truth — honest question, handshaking, honest answer deserved and expected.

"Didn't hear it from her myself, Cal," I told him. "But the rumor I heard was, she said it. She likes the Mayor better than you, because his is bigger — don't feel bad, Cal, so what? We can't all have a sizable *BRAIN*."

I thought then he might *really* shoot me — but instead, he busted out laughing.

"His *brain!*" cried Pettygore then. Tears of laughter ran from his eyes, and blood leaked from a corner of his mouth as he punched my arm, almost friendly. "Oh, Frakes, that's a good one alright. You sure had me going for awhile. She likes the Mayor for his big *brain!*"

CHAPTER 46
TOFFEES AND TURNIPS

"Thought we was gonna ignore the Mayor and Sheriff til later," Wally said as me and Mary walked up to him and Georgina. "You didn't let nothin' slip, did you?"

Mary didn't catch on, but I heard Georgina's quick mind all a'ticking and a'clicking as she weighed up Wally's words.

"Don't know what you mean, young Mister Davis," I replied. "Dang skunk Sheriff cheated me, pretended to sneeze to ruin my shot."

The adoring look on little Mary's face woulda been worth putting in bottles. "You'd *never* have missed otherwise, would you, Father?"

"Maybe not," I replied. "It *was* windy down there though, more so than over here. Mighty fine shootist that young kid that won it. Looked some familiar to me too."

The tables and such had already been moved, as the horses for the next race made their way to the start.

Georgina sent Mary to watch the race from down near the finish line, and gave her some money to buy herself a mountain of toffee once race five was over.

Soon as the child skipped away, smile on face and money in hand, Georgina laid out her cards. "Alright, I know I said I'd leave it to you, but I've waited long enough for the truth. If there's danger, I need to know. Mary's been through enough."

Me and Wally looked at each other, but there weren't no way outta telling her. Right away, I had Wally fill her in on where we was at with our plan.

She took it all in her stride — she was used to me after all a'these years, and she wanted to catch these skunks out just as much as I did.

"Are we certain Delvene isn't here?" she asked. "A mother has more influence than you may know, and if we could get her to speak to her sons—"

"She ain't here," I said. "Then again, she might turn up late, just in time for their race. But I doubt it, she dislikes the racing. Still, it ain't far to come — keep a lookout for her if you want."

I didn't think it would help, and Wally was against saying anything to her at all — but in the end we agreed that Georgina and Mary should keep an eye out for the woman, and if they found her, Georgina and me would have a word with her in private.

A twenty-to-one outsider won the fifth race, and Mary returned with an even bigger smile than expected.

"Musta been mighty fine toffee," I said. "You look like a cat that found a whole bucket a'cream."

"Oh," she replied. "That's right, toffee. I forgot all about that." Then her eyes lit right up and she said, "Did you hear the magnificent name of the winner of that race? It was Mayblossom Girl! You know, just like my wonderful doll, Princess Mayblossom. I asked Mister Deputy Emmett to put a bet on her for me. I *know* I should not *really* have bet all my toffee money — but look, I won ten whole dollars! Oh, look, here he comes now, and he has Handsome Roy with him too."

We made a fuss of her win, a'course. *Even Georgina.* Ain't every day someone wins on a bet at twenty-to-one — but we had to get down to business, there weren't much time, and we had to be quick about it.

Georgina took Mary to go buy us all some refreshments, and left all us men to discuss how we might catch the skunks out and ruin their plans. It wouldn't be easy, and would require some quite exact timing — but we was all on the same page, with a shared common goal.

When we'd finished discussing the plan and we all understood what our part in it was, young Roy brought up something that surprised us.

Seemed obvious once Roy said it, but if logic was logical, it'd be called a turnip, and no one would know what it was — well, I know that don't make no sense, but my Grandpa sure seemed to enjoy himself when he said it, and it does make you think.

"I know you don't wish to upset Mary," Roy said, "but if you're so sure this whole thing's about horses and ring-ins, should you not have asked her if her parents ever owned a racehorse, or at least knew the Abbotts somehow?

Might be they was involved in it up to their ears, and the child might recall somethin' helpful."

I explained that Delvene already told us she never knew the Wilsons — but a'course, that didn't mean her husband and sons hadn't met 'em one way or another.

"And the Abbotts *did* already own a Livery," Roy pointed out. "You really should at least *ask* Mary if they ever bought a horse or a buggy or any such thing from in town."

I don't know if anyone else felt it, but my skin crawled around on my bones then, and I *knew* Roy was right — we *should* talk to Mary about her parents and horses.

But still, I was reluctant — she had been acting strangely at times, this past couple of days. Could not be easy for the child, I'd rather not push her.

I told them all so, but promised I'd talk to her later — or perhaps get Georgina to do so. To a man, they all agreed that it should be Georgina.

We all went our separate ways then, not wishing to be seen together too long, like as if we was cooking up something.

And talking to Mary *could* wait until later. The plan we had was a good one — we would catch them all out on ringing in a horse in the Cup, and hope that the truth of the murders would come out after that, once they was in jail.

If it went well, them skunks would all be arrested a couple of hours from now — if it didn't, we might be in trouble ourselves. Also, Emmett might lose his job. But the risk was well worth it, all of us was agreed.

And if we won big on the horse race, it'd be a nice bonus.

CHAPTER 47

MARY, SILENTLY SLEUTHING

When Mother suggested we leave Father and the other men to talk, I just *knew* that something was up. I may be just a young girl, but it's not only *books* that I read — reading *faces* can teach us so much!

And the little exchanges of looks between Mother and Father, and all the others too, told me beyond doubt there was more to their planned conversation than only racehorses.

They must know WHO killed my parents! Or WHY are they engaging in all this secretive — let's say surreptitious, an even better word for it — behavior!

And PERHAPS the threatening letter I'd found had something to do with all that!

Of *course*, Mother isn't a fool. She could tell I suspected something, even though all the men missed it.

I'm quite certain she can read minds — I *know* she reads Father's sometimes — and she saw right through my plan to escape her, so I could sneak behind the horse stalls and secretly listen to the men speaking.

She even went so far as to take me to the betting ring to check the odds on the horses for the next race, as well as the Cup. And I *know* she has no interest in betting! It wasn't until she was distracted by a lovely matronly woman in an overlarge hat that was covered in *all* sorts of feathers, that I was able to slip away from her, and rush back to listen to Father's secretive talk!

I was *almost* too late! By the time I worked out where they were — I *should have counted how many steps it was out the front, then walked that many steps at the BACK* — it seemed Father and his friends were about to part ways.

It was difficult to hear, and I could not make out every word — but Handsome Roy said *something* about racehorses, and something about my parents perhaps knowing the *Abbotts*.

The general consensus was, that *I* should be interviewed about it, to ascertain whether my parents indeed knew the Abbotts.

The plot thickens!

It seems they suspect that the Abbotts know the true identity of Jesse Gillespie!

Could the BROTHERS have participated in murder most foul? Surely not! They seem such lovely young men.

And yet...

SOMEONE *wrote that note, telling Father he must leave Cheyenne or we all would be killed.*

I MUST investigate!

I had not seen the Abbott brothers all day, but of *course*

— it was just simple logic — they *must* be guarding their horses.

I drew my collar up to my ears, and sneaked in a manner most stealthy, searching them out. Finally my silent sleuthing paid off — their horses were stabled two rows behind Mister Wally's. They were *almost* at the very far end of the row, farthest from the grandstand and betting ring, with no other horses or people close by.

Perhaps if I sneaked up unnoticed, and secreted myself in the stable next door, I might hear them speak of Jesse Gillespie! Who knows? It was worth a try.

I waited alongside the end stable, the vacant one right next to theirs. There was a *colossal* pile of straw inside it, just what I needed, a good place to hide — and suddenly, both Abbott brothers rose from their chairs and walked forward, looked down the hill for some reason. So while their attention was elsewhere, I nipped around, quiet as an infinitesimal mouse, and ducked down behind the straw pile, and I *listened*.

I very nearly cried out as I ducked down, for a rat the size of an *antelope* scurried into the pile of straw, not an arm's length away from my face!

Goodness, I just DETEST rats!

The Abbott brothers came back to their chairs after just a few moments, and began to chat, just as I'd hoped they would.

During that first couple of minutes, I learned *only* three things:

One; the brother called Clarrie is sweet on a girl called

Delilah — and if they earn enough money today, he's going to ask her to marry him.

Two; the other brother, Ben, believes Clarrie is a fool if he thinks a pretty girl like Delilah will say yes to him. I found it *exceedingly* difficult not to speak at that moment — *I needed to tell Ben not to be mean* — but somehow I stayed quiet.

And finally, the number three thing I discovered by listening; *both* young men are *terrified* of the horrid Mayor Fisk, as you will now hear.

"Here comes the damn Mayor," Ben hissed at his brother. "Stand up, make like you're busy."

"Dammit," Clarrie replied. "At least he's alone and unarmed."

"He carries a derringer, fool." I heard the crunch of both brothers' feet on the gravel out front of the stall, then Ben said, "He won't hurt no one today — leastways, not as long as the horse wins and nothin' goes wrong."

After that they went silent a few moments, and I crouched down even further, trying to quiet my heartbeat so they wouldn't hear me.

Then they greeted the Mayor, who replied to their pleasant greetings with only meanness.

"This best go as planned, or you two know what will happen. Is the color set right?"

Did I HEAR that correctly?

What an ODD thing to say!

"Of course it is, Mister Fisk, sir. I mean Mayor, sir. Mayor Fisk, a'course, what I meant. Long as there ain't no rain we're home free. You bribe the official who checks all the markings?"

"If by bribe, you mean *threatened his life* — then yes, of course I did. I'm not a *fool*, you know, Abbott! Do *you* think me foolish?"

"No, Mister Fisk, Mayor," said Clarrie. "I think you're—"

"I'm still worried 'bout the Davis horse, sir," Ben said. "I know ours is ready, but Light of My Life won with a *heap* in reserve last week up in Sidney. And everyone knows how good ol' Wally Davis can train."

"Not a problem," the Mayor replied. "Despite all the *incompetence* displayed by the fools I've employed up til now, we've had *one* stroke of luck. The jockey whom Davis has employed for the Cup has agreed — for a rather large sum, which will come out of *your* share, you fools—"

"But that ain't—"

"Sounds fair enough," Ben hurriedly said. "Please go on, Mayor Fisk, and don't pay Clarrie no mind, he's just nervous is all."

"He'd better snap out of that," that *mean* Mayor replied. "I've paid Davis's jockey to mess up the start, find himself trapped in the ruck, go wide at the turn, and do anything else that's required to *not* win the race. In short, our mare cannot be beaten!"

Unfortunately, I was *so* shocked at hearing those words, a gasp escaped from my lips!

And I'm quite certain YOU'D have gasped too, well of course you would, wouldn't you!

The problem my gasp caused was twofold — and both problems were *rats*.

Firstly, my gasp caused the ugly rat in the straw to appear at the edge of the pile to see what was happening. This startled me *more,* but I bit my tongue and tried not to scream — which was *not* at all easy, and took *all* of my self-control!

The horrid thing sat there staring at me, twitching his nose and deciding whether to bite me — a most *terrifying* experience, I can assure you!

But secondly — this part even worse — the uglier, meaner, more *dangerous* rat: to wit, the horrid Mayor Reginald Fisk, was alerted to my presence in the stable, just ten feet from where he now stood!

"What was that?" he growled. "Get your guns, you damn fools, there's someone in that horse-box listening."

"We don't *got* guns," Ben replied, and he sounded quite terrified. "I sure hope they don't neither."

"Get in there and get after him," hissed the Mayor. "You flush the man out and I'll shoot the damn spy with my Derringer."

In that horrific, terrifying moment I *knew* I was done for — I would *surely* be cut down in my youth, be denied all the joys of adulthood: the wonderment of falling in love; having children of my own; making a happy, beautiful life with my own true love and...

Oh, wait, I thought then. *Just DO something, Mary! DO something!*

To be honest, it took no thought at all — the rat near my feet had turned his attention from me to the men outside, and as he twitched his nose and began to turn around to dart back into the straw, I *kicked* the nasty thing as hard as I could! It squealed and flew a short way, landed at the edge of the open stable and ran away, *ran* for its life!

"Oh, damn," Ben Abbott said with a sigh of relief. "It was only a *rat*. I sure do hate rats, don't you, Mister Mayor?"

And the Mayor said, "You fools, it was only a rat." And I heard his angry footsteps as he walked away, before he turned and called, "Just make certain nothing goes wrong, or you *know* what will happen! Torturous, horrible deaths, I can *promise* you that! You two first — then your *mother!*"

CHAPTER 48
GEORGINA STEPS UP

"Calm down, Mary, please," I said, grasping the child by her shoulders to steady her some. "Now speak slow and clear, we can't understand what you're saying."

"Take a breath, dear," said Georgina, as she stroked Mary's hair to soothe her. "And now ... nice and slow, tell us."

"He plans to hurt dear Mrs Abbott," Mary said, after ceasing her sobbing. Sure didn't talk no slower though — her next words tumbled on out of her twenty-at-least-to-the-dozen. "And there was a rat, a big nasty rat, and the Mayor is so mean, and the jockey, oh, Mister Wally, he's already bribed your jockey, and I thought I'd be killed, and please, Father, please, you *must* do something quickly, oh, *please!*"

It took a minute or two to calm the child down well enough to answer our questions, but when she managed it, we sure did learn some things.

"So we know it for certain," said Wally. "And we know they've used color *today*. Just hope I can tell where, and it ain't on the face."

Mary looked at him, dumbstruck, when he said it. "What*ever* are you speaking of, Mister Wally? Of *all* the things I just told you, the one that makes no sense at all is the one that you *seize* upon? And then you talk *gibberish* about it, oh, what a strange, unfortunate day!"

"You're a genius, Mary," he told her. "There ain't time to explain, but you are. You done good alright, child, *real* good. But for right now, you'll just have to trust us, we got things to do and no time to explain 'em, alright?"

"Well ... yes, I suppose," Mary answered, and Georgina said, "Good girl, Mary, let's keep quiet now and listen."

"You'll need another jockey for starters," I said. "And you still ain't in no condition, young Wally, don't try to tell me you are. That was race six that just finished, there ain't much time."

"I ain't got no choice," Wally said. "And though I'm well over the weight, I think we can still finish second, and that'll be enough."

"Only if we can prove what they've done," I said. "And besides, the way we made the plan needs *you* to be on foot when the jockeys mount up in the yard. No one else has a decent excuse to pull off what you got planned."

"What*ever* are you on about?" little Mary asked — but immediately she waved it away and said, "Sorry, time's of the essence, I forgot for a moment."

"I forgot about that, Lyle," Wally said. "But there's no one can ride Lulu to victory — no one I can *trust* anyway."

And right then, to Wally's great surprise, Georgina said, "Wally. You can trust *me*. I'll ride your mare, and we'll win."

We all of us let it hang there in the breeze some long moments — seemed like an age anyway.

Wally was shaking his head, a little sadly perhaps, and he finally said, "Georgina Frakes. You're a courageous, intelligent woman, and I'd trust you with my life — which is to say, I'd trust you with my horses."

"I can do it, Wally. Trust me."

"I already *did* trust you, having you ride Lulu out at your place — that little canter we went on, you me and Mary. But I can't have you risking your neck — this race ain't no canter, it's more like a war when a Cup race gets to the turn and the big money's on."

Georgina stared at Wally a few quiet moments, weighing up what he had said, then she turned to me. "Lyle, *you* tell him. I don't think he understands. Tell our friend here the *truth* — he'll listen to you."

All around us, the hustle and bustle of a busy race day went on. But in our little bubble we heard nothing of it, and everything quietened, the way it does right before a gunfight, when *All hell breaks loose,* just for one way to put it.

"Wally," I said into the silence, as his eyes studied mine for some sign of doubt or tomfoolery. "You're the best man with a horse I ever saw. But you're only the second-best rider — the best rider I ever saw just made you an offer. And though she ain't a spring chicken, and that out there *will* be a battle — there ain't no one I know who I'd trust any better to bring your horse home a winner. But it's up to you to decide."

Wally searched Georgina's eyes, another long moment. And whatever it was that passed between them right then was a thing that must only be known to the truest of horsemen, horsewomen and horses — for it meant nothing to me — and when Wally looked away, looked around at his horse then looked back, I was sure he'd say *No*.

But instead, young Wally Davis said, "Lyle, go with her, tell the Stewards the rider's been changed again. Tell 'em it's Georgina Frakes now, and do all the paperwork. Go now, quick as you can, there ain't much time."

CHAPTER 49
"A WOMAN RIDE IN A HORSE RACE...?"

When we told the Chief Steward the new rider's name, the besuited, overfed skunk leaned back in his chair and laughed in our faces.

"Haha, that's a good one," he said, his double chins wobbling fit to cause someone an injury if they got too close. "A *woman* ride in a horse race — and the *Cup* race no less?"

"Something amuse you?" I said, making a fist I quite wanted to use — and though the man was still laughing it weren't quite so loud now.

Georgina put her small hand on my forearm, and I knew she was right to do so, a'course, but my dander had sure been disturbed, and the feller now noticed.

He put down his pencil, clasped his hands in front of him like he was praying and said, "My apologies, sir. I thought my assistant had sent you in to say all that as a sort of a joke. A little *jest,* if you may. He's a practical joker, you see, and comes up with some good ones from time to time. But ... hmmm ... you *seem* to be serious."

Georgina smiled that smile a'hers, the one that makes strangers fall over 'emselves just to help her, no matter the problem. "Mister Truefellow, isn't it? There isn't much time, and there *was* a rumor that a certain jockey had been persuaded to not do his best."

"That's a *serious* accusation, Madame! Where did you hear it, I must know immediately. We don't take such things lightly, I promise, I'll get to the facts or so help me—"

"There is no *proof,* Mister Truefellow, it was only a rumor that reached Mister Davis's ears. It may not be true at all — but what *is* true, and what you must act on, is that Mister Davis sent *us* along to inform you that *I* will be riding the horse."

The man's mouth fell open like he was an overweight fish outta water, the moment she told him that. *"You,* Madame? *You?* Surely not. Why, you must be..."

Well, that feller's words trailed off and his eyes went from disbelieving to *what-have-I-said* in roundabout half a second — just like *every* other man who almost insulted a woman by stating his unasked-for opinion of her age.

I sure was glad I weren't him, right about then.

Georgina narrowed her eyes, lifted one eyebrow and said, "I must be *what,* hmmm? *Cold,* perhaps, were you going to say? Too *hungry* to ride, was it then? Or perhaps you were merely going to point out that I look too *heavy* to ride the horse at the weight? *Which* of these was it, sir? Hmmm?"

Them hands a'his went from prayer-like to *please-*

don't-attack-me, I-wish-I-was-somewhere-else-now. Way he held 'em outstretched in front of him, palms toward us, I reckon he hoped they'd block whatever bullets her eyes fired.

"Oh, *no,* Madame, I meant none of those things," he said, "or anything else untoward. I was *merely* enquiring whether you had your paperwork filled in yet. But of course, I would have it already, how *perfectly* stupid of me. Here," he said, opening his desk drawer and fishing out a blank sheet of paper, which he placed before her. "Name, address, and ... oh, dear, I'm not sure how to put this, but..."

"It's quite alright," she told him, smiling that smile again. "You're a *gentleman,* sir, I can tell. And I know you would *never* ask a woman her age — but rules being rules, I will, of course, write it on the paper. Is that *all* you require?"

"Yes, Madame, it is. And I thank you sincerely for being so understanding. And Madame?

"Yes?"

"Jolly good luck for the race."

CHAPTER 50

SEEING A GHOST

A short time later, as Georgina and me were walking back to the stables, the announcer told the crowd that the jockey had been changed *again*, for Light of My Life, the Davis-trained horse.

"What's the *meaning* of this?" boomed a voice from the grandstand nearby — the voice of Mayor Reginald Fisk.

But when the announcer said the new jockey's name was Mrs Georgina Frakes, that damn fool Fisk busted out laughing.

We stopped and glared up at the fool, and noticing us there, he raised his voice even higher.

"An *old woman* riding a horse in the Cup? For one thing, it cannot be legal. For another, it's the most foolish thing I ever heard. Davis must know he can't win — he's using the ancient crone as his jockey, so he has an excuse for being beaten so far by my own mare. What a *fool* this man Davis must be! The woman must be seventy-five!"

Now, I know my wife's true age, and it's got a five at the

start of it — also, she don't look nowhere near her right age, for she's strong and healthy and beautiful as most thirty-year-olds, or my name ain't Frakes — but when the fool said what he did, I thought, *Here we go, she might get locked up and not get to ride, what she's about to do to the skunk.*

But Georgina only smiled at me, said, "Let everyone think I'm that old, we'll get better odds," and she walked away with that smile only growing — and indeed, she affected a limp as she walked, and somehow gave a frail impression.

Me, I never said a word.

But it seemed like everyone else on that dang racecourse did — and it mostly weren't kind.

Still, it worked just how she'd hoped.

"Six-to-one, Light of My Life," called a bookmaker as we went past, then another called, "Sevens! How about it, Mister Frakes? Not even you will show some support for your wife?"

"My money's on The Dark Horse," I lied. "No use gettin' sentimental when it comes to bets."

Somehow I walked away from the seven-to-one that was offered, and behind us all we could hear was *The Dark Horse, The Dark Horse, The Dark Horse.*

When we got back young Wally was checking on his concoctions. "Just making sure it's the right bucket," he said, as Roy Grimm brought out the Cup mare and walked her around some.

Emmett Slaughter was there too, having decided to escort the horse to the parade yard, just in case them skunks still had more tricks up their sleeves.

A few minutes later, down in the parade yard itself, Roy was walking Light of My Life around the big circle with all a'the others. All but one had arrived — the Abbott-trained mare, The Dark Horse, owned by Reginald Fisk.

"They'll hide her until the last possible moment," said Wally. "But she'll appear any moment. One more minute, then she'll be a scratching, they sure are cutting it fine."

Wally and Georgina stood just inside of the fence, and I stood outside it, watching on. Young Emmett was watching from nearby in the betting ring, while Mary was standing close to him, along with the orphanage owner, the lovely Mavis Benson, who had arrived just in time for the Cup race.

I waved to them, and they waved right back — and then came the booming voice of the announcer. **"HERE SHE IS NOW, THE HEAVILY BACKED ONE-TO-TWO FAVORITE — THE DARK HORSE — OWNED BY THE HONORABLE MAYOR OF CHEYENNE, OUR VERY OWN REGINALD FISK — WHAT A BEAUTIFUL SPECIMEN SHE IS, FOLKS — HER RECENT FORM HAS BEEN POOR, BUT JUST LOOK AT THAT STRENGTH!"**

"Well blow me down with a feather and walk on my grave," Wally said, as he watched the young Abbott brothers bring the mare through the gate and trot her into the parade yard.

"What is it, Wally?" I said. "You look like you just seen a ghost."

"I reckon I have," he said quietly. Then he whispered to me, "Look at the size a'those ears! It's her, Lyle, it's Jessy

Gillespie. I'd know her anywhere, she's somethin' special alright. The fools have brought her along. We have them. We *have* them."

I looked across to where Emmett stood, and when he took off his hat, I took off mine too.

Simple signals the best, such circumstances.

He looked away, put his hat back on, went about his business, just like as if nothing had happened.

"Where's the color, Wally?" I whispered as I turned back to him.

"Right where I knew it would be, if it was her. It's her forelegs they've colored. Jessy's are actually white. It's a good job, but I think the dye will come off if we get this right. We have them, Lyle — we *have* them."

There was only two mares in the race — Light of My Life and The Dark Horse, a'course — so in the field of twelve, they was numbers eleven and twelve. Wally's horse was eleven.

The proximity of them two numbers meant Georgina and Wally was stood next to where the Abbott boys were as they waited. Roy was walking Wally's horse round the parade yard as a warmup — and the Mayor himself was now leading his own horse around, playing to the gallery while the Abbott boys anxiously watched.

"Shouldn't train for outside owners, young fellers," Wally said to them. "They'll get you in all sorts a'trouble with all their big schemes and ideas. That's why I only train for myself. Nice horse, by the way. Looks plenty fitter'n she did last week, you musta done somethin' ... *different* ... in how you trained her. Well, good luck I guess, boys — you're gonna need it."

When Wally said the word *different,* them boys looked like they wished the ground would open up and swaller 'em whole.

But one of 'em just gave a nod and the other said, "Good luck to you too, Mister Davis. And I almost forgot, our Ma said to send her regards."

"And to her," Wally said. "Though I'm sure I'll be seeing her soon — I'll be seeing you *all* soon."

He leaned on his walking stick, limped about every so often as the horses paraded. Then when it was time for the jockeys to mount, the Mayor handed the reins of The Dark Horse to one of the Abbotts, as the other stood by — and Wally made his move.

As he walked toward his own horse, with his his walking stick in one hand and his bucket of *"vitamin water"* in the other, Wally Davis lost his balance, fell sideways — and threw that special bucketful of *"vitamin water"* all over the forelegs of The Dark Horse.

Or rather, Jessy Gillespie.

As Wally crashed to the ground, he was wearing a smile. He'd hit her just right.

The horse nickered, stamped her feet nervous-like, and young Clarrie Abbott cried out, "Careful there, Mister Davis, you spilled it all over our horse. Shhh, good girl, Petal, settle down now, it's alright."

The fool Mayor was so busy big-noting himself, he never even noticed what happened.

"I'm so sorry, young feller," said Wally, as the other

young Abbott — the jockey called Ben — helped him onto his feet.

"Just water with vitamins in it," said Wally. "Real sorry, boys, you best rub that water off her. Can't have you gettin' an unfair advantage, my liquids cooling your horse on the way to the start line."

Both them Abbotts looked wide-eyed at Wally, then both spun and looked at the legs of the horse — she was soaked almost up to where her forelegs met up with her shoulders.

Both boys looked about to see if Mayor Fisk had been watching — and they both looked alarmed.

"I ain't got a towel," Clarrie said, mighty panicked.

"Something wrong, boys?" Wally asked, pulling out an oversize kerchief and offering it to them. "I was just joking about the advantage. You should wipe off the water though, I reckon. What you lookin' to the owner for? He knows less about horses than a rock does."

"Stand between us in case he looks round," said Clarrie Abbott. His brother Ben moved quick to block Mayor Fisk's view of the horse, while Clarrie rubbed at the water with the kerchief Wally had handed him.

When they thought back on this moment later, they'd realize they just made it worse — rubbing the horsehair with the kerchief was *not* the right thing to do. It made the vitamins and baking soda in Wally's concoction loosen the walnut dye only all the much faster.

CHAPTER 51
"AND THEY'RE AWAY!"

Just before Roy legged Georgina up on the horse, Wally gave her his final instructions.

"Don't try to lead, keep her calm. Hold her back, keep her outside of the ruck. And when you get to the back straight take her out wide. I got a little secret up my sleeve — I paid an enterprising young feller who works here to connect up the watering system and flood the inside running over where the public can't see. He's been doing just a little all day, but the past forty minutes he's turned the rails running over there into a lake."

Georgina stared at him in disbelief. "Isn't that dangerous?"

"The other jockeys already know it's wet there. It's just a lot wetter now. They know to be careful, and no one will be going quick that early in running." Then he smiled a wry one and added, "It's to water the legs of the horses, keep 'em all nice and cool."

"Wally Davis," she said. "You mean one horse in

particular, don't you? The one you already poured water on."

He smiled, leaned over to speak into her ear. "You don't have to beat The Dark Horse, and you probably won't. Second will get us the money. Them front legs a'hers is gonna have walnut dye runnin' all over her hooves by the time she gets back. Work our Lulu into the race round the bend, take off at the top a'the straight, let her do the rest. Trust her, she knows what she's doing."

"Look everyone, the foolish *woman's* forgotten her whip," the loathsome Mayor yelled to the crowd with a laugh. "Oh, this is going to be a fine day, let me tell you. Bet big, my people of Cheyenne. This is my gift to you!"

"Whips ain't necessary for horses properly trained," Wally replied. "Though I'd be happy to use one on *you,* you dang loudmouthed fool. Gift to the people *indeed.* See you after the race, you filthy dang bush-rat."

As Georgina and Light of My Life made their way to the start, we all went to the betting ring.

"Eight-to-one odds if you'd like them, Mister Davis," the nearest bookmaker cried out.

"Don't mind if I do," Wally replied, and took out a roll of cash the size of a fist. "Five-hundred alright?"

"Four-thousand to five-hundred," the greedy-eyed bookmaker replied, and his clerk wrote it down on the ticket, and also into the book.

By the time we'd gone right round the betting ring putting more bets on, we stood to win twenty-thousand dollars between us, and the race was about to get started.

"THEY'RE ALL LINING UP — THE DARK HORSE

LOOKS FRACTIOUS — SHE SETTLES — AND THEY'RE
AWAY!"

They started at the top of the straight, ran down past
the grandstand at a slow lope, passed us at the finish line
with a full lap to go.

Georgina had bounced Light of My Life out nice and
straight, but took a tight hold on the reins to settle her down
running eighth of the twelve — right next to The Dark
Horse in seventh. As they made the gentle left turn, the
field sorted themselves into six pairs of two, nose-to-tail,
nose-to-tail.

Georgina kept Light of My Life just outside The Dark
Horse, but as they went down the back stretch they finally
separated a little.

"THE DARK HORSE IN SEVENTH, FIVE LENGTHS
FROM THE LEAD, GOING WELL," we heard from the
announcer. "AND DROPPING OFF A LITTLE NOW,
RUNNING WIDE ON THE TRACK IS THE DAVIS HORSE,
LIGHT OF MY LIFE — IT APPEARS WOMAN JOCKEYS
CANNOT KEEP THEIR HORSES CONTROLLED, SHE'S
RUNNING TOO WIDE!"

Then through my spyglass I saw the sheets of water
that rose from the other eleven horses, as they strode
through the wet section, one hundred yards worth,
splashing up near all their faces!

They'd all slowed by the time they came to it — all
except for Light of My Life, who continued on at her same
loping pace.

As they came to the start of the turn, Light of My Life

was third, up on the outside, and doing it easy, only two lengths from the leaders.

The Dark Horse had dropped back as they went through the wet, and was now ten lengths behind Georgina's mount, running last, and not looking good.

"That Jessy don't look much to me," I said to Wally.

But he only said, "Just keep watching, she's something special, though she don't much like water — but it ain't over yet, just keep your eyes peeled, you'll see!"

A half-mile from the finish, a great roar erupted from the crowd, as the words most were hoping to hear burst out from the giant voice-trumpet.

"AND NOW THE DARK HORSE TAKES OFF — MAKING A MOVE FROM THE REAR OF THE FIELD — SHE'S TENTH — NOW SHE'S EIGHTH — AND THE DARK HORSE IS RUNNING AT DOUBLE THE SPEED OF THE OTHERS."

"Young Abbott's took off too hard and too early," cried Wally. "Even *she* can't sprint home the half-mile, and she'll be forced out wide!"

When they turned into the home stretch, Georgina gave her horse its head, and she raced to the leaders in a stride and set sail for home.

"Go, Mother," cried Mary as she leaned out over the outside rail of the racecourse. *"Go, Lulu, go!"*

The roar of the crowd almost lifted us up off our feet, it was deafening now — yet somehow, impossibly louder, came the excited tones of the announcer.

"LIGHT OF MY LIFE IS THE LEADER, RUNNING AWAY BY FOUR LENGTHS FROM THE TIRING BANJO — BUT

HERE COMES THE DARK HORSE — THE DARK HORSE SIX LENGTHS FROM THE LEADER, BUT LOOK AT HER FLY!"

Georgina, her feet up high in short stirrups, so unlike how the other jockeys rode, moved with the horse as if part of it — and they sure *was* moving, like a beautiful painting that suddenly turned into flesh and thundered toward us, impossibly perfect, unbelievably so.

And yet, The Dark Horse came on faster.

"AT THE FURLONG, LIGHT OF MY LIFE BY A LENGTH — BUT THE DARK HORSE GOES TO HER, THE DARK HORSE — LIGHT — DARK — THE LIGHT — THE DARK — NOW THE DARK HORSE IN FRONT BY A NECK, AND NOW A HALF-LENGTH, SHE'S GOT IT, SHE'S GOT IT!"

"Not yet she ain't," Wally cried. "Keep at it, girl, GO!"

Stride for stride they ate up the ground, and just as Wally said, a half-mile sprint was too much — even for the wonderful Jessy Gillespie, who finally tired, as Georgina urged her horse on.

"Go Mother, go," Mary cried as they thundered past us, just a few yards away — and Light of My Life refused to give in, got herself equal again, got her head in front of The Dark Horse, and it was all over.

"LIGHT OF MY LIFE IS TOO GOOD, SHE BEATS THE DARK HORSE BY A NECK — WHAT A RACE, WHAT A RACE, WHAT A RACE — AND TEN LENGTHS TO BOUNTIFUL BUDDY, A GOOD RUN FOR THIRD."

CHAPTER 52
A MYSTERY EXPLAINED

As the jockeys slowed down their horses to a light canter, then brought them to a stop, I seen young Ben Abbott reach over and offer Georgina his hand.

"Well done, Mrs Frakes," she later told me he'd said. "I think I ain't got long to live, so now's the best time to say it. That was *some* ride, Ma'am."

Then the crowd — which had gone from a great booming roar to a murmur of mostly shocked silence — rose up into a roar again.

Or rather, as Mary worded it, *"A veritable cacophony of ululations and vociferations."*

"A vestibule cackling of what, child?" I yelled in her ear.

"Howls and hollers," she called back, with a pleased little smile.

Then I heard with my own ears what the crowd was all

on about — we'd missed it first time, due to all of our own celebrations and jumpings for joy.

"YES, FOLKS, I NOW HAVE CONFIRMATION — THE RACE FINISH JUDGE, IN HIS WISDOM, HAD DECLARED THE RESULT A DEAD-HEAT — PENDING CORRECT WEIGHT OF COURSE — BUT FOR NOW, PLEASE HOLD ALL BETTING TICKETS."

Well a'course, some folks in the crowd there was mighty relieved, having bet on The Dark Horse — a dead-heat means you get half the money your betting ticket's worth, as *both* horses win half the prize each. But the surprising thing was, even some of the men who'd bet on The Dark Horse was voicing their absolute disgust.

I felt a great respect for those men.

Important thing, honor.

There was jeers and catcalls aplenty, and angry shoutings of *"CHEATS!"* and *"A RORT!"*

Thing is, that race finish judge woulda had to be blind not to see Wally's mare had won clearly — and everyone on the course knew it. And speaking of judges, ol' Judge Wilcott looked at the race finish judge with such anger, I reckon the feller might shoulda just started runnin'. He's straight as a blade, ol' Judge Wilcott, and doubly dangerous to men who do the wrong thing.

As we struggled through the crowd to the fence of the Parade Yard, Georgina and the other jockeys were coming back in to go get 'emselves weighed.

They would not allow me and Mary through the gate with Wally at first, then he told the feller we was the actual owners of the winner, and he waved us through into the yard.

The damn Mayor came down from the grandstand, waving like he was some hero at a parade that was made in his honor. Well, he soon realized that weren't *quite* how folks felt — someone with a real good throwing arm fired a rotten tomato at Fisk's ugly head, and that feller was a mighty good shot.

Overripe tomato splattered from beeswax to breakfast-time, some of it landing on Sheriff Cal Pettygore's face when it bounced off the Mayor.

To cries of *Cheats, Rort and Thieves,* the Sheriff and Mayor — *both men were now waving their guns about to keep people away from them* — made their way to the gate and came through into the Parade Yard.

"Thought you had me there for a moment," the skunk Mayor said to Wally, with a dung-eating grin.

I just about leaped at him then, but Wally put his arm across my body and, with a smile someone shoulda painted, said, "But we *do* have you, Mister Mayor. We have you *right* where we want you."

As young Roy Grimm held the bridle, my beautiful muddy-faced wife climbed down from Light of My Life, just five yards away from us, where we stood behind a rope. I smiled at Georgina and said, "Best rider I ever saw — and that the best ride. You did it, Princess, you won — no filthy lying race judge can take away the truth, and all who saw the race know it."

"I agree," Wally said with a nod. "Good a ride as I ever saw, and I've seen the best."

"She was *wonderful,* wasn't she?" said Mary, looking at Georgina adoringly. "You were wonderful, Mother! And so was our dear equine friend, our beautiful Lulu! She lights up *all* of our lives!"

We weren't allowed near Georgina, a'course — rules state no one can touch the jockeys before they unsaddle their horses and step on the scales to weigh in.

Georgina was then led away by the Chief Steward, to step on the weighing scales, carrying the tiny saddle she'd used for the race.

As the *much* muddier Ben Abbott climbed down from The Dark Horse, we were joined in the Parade Yard by three new arrivals — Deputy Emmett Slaughter had brought the two Federal Marshals assigned to the traveling horse-race carnival.

Emmett was pointing to The Dark Horse's front feet and legs — there was streaky patches of white showing through all the brown, and brown color running down onto that fine horse's hooves.

"What's all *this* then?" Wally said, smiling at the skunk Mayor. "Looks like we got a ring-in, no wonder her speed improved so. Oldest trick in the book, walnut dye is ya dang fool!" Then to the Abbotts he said, "This don't happen when you train for yourself, boys. You'd best tell the truth now, I reckon, or it's long jail terms for you both."

As one Federal Marshal bent down, wiped some dye off the horse with a finger and tasted it — *no idea why he'd do such a thing* — the other Marshal took out his sidearm and pointed it at the Mayor.

"I do believe we need to talk, sir," he said. "Mayor

Reginald Fisk, you are under arrest on suspicion of committing a financial fraud on a racecourse."

Fisk gripped the upper arm of the Sheriff beside him. "Do something, Cal, damn you, *do* something!"

Sheriff Cal Pettygore summed it all up in an instant, his gaze shrewdly moving from the Marshal to the horse, then to me then back to the Marshal. He slapped his old friend on the back and said, "You're on your own, Reg."

"Do something, Cal, *dammit,*" cried Fisk, taking his gun from his waistcoat and pointing it first at the Sheriff, then at Wally, and then at the Marshal. "I'll take you down with me, Cal, I'll tell—"

Cal Pettygore musta seen his life explode into flame then, and he acted fast. As Fisk said the words *'take you down'* Cal leaped behind the Mayor, grabbed him in a headlock and commenced then to punch the man's face for all he was worth.

The crowd sure was getting their money's worth for the day — as Pettygore kept up his punching, the crowd called out *all* sorts a'things. Mostly *Hit the damn skunk, Hit him harder,* and *Give him one for me, the damn cheat.*

Seemed the citizens of Cheyenne did not take too kindly to cheats — or perhaps they just didn't like being told to bet on a sure thing, then seeing it beat fair and square.

More-or-less fair and square, anyway — the matter of the water along the back straight comes to mind, now I think some about it.

As one Federal Marshal took hold of the bleeding

Mayor Reginald Fisk, the other ordered the Abbotts to wash all the color off of the legs of The Dark Horse.

As they attended to that, out boomed the announcement that made us all wealthier — **"CORRECT WEIGHT ON NUMBER ELEVEN — THE WINNER IS ELEVEN, LIGHT OF MY LIFE — BOOKMAKERS MAY NOW PAY OUT — NUMBER TWELVE, THE DARK HORSE IS DISQUALIFIED, BUT DECLARED AS A RUNNER — NO REFUNDS ON LOSING BETS — BOOKMAKERS ALL CLEAR TO PAY OUT ON LIGHT OF MY LIFE — AND ALL PATRONS ARE INVITED TO WATCH THE CUP PRESENTATION TO THE WINNERS."**

As the Abbotts washed the brown off of Jessy Gillespie's forelegs, the Federal Marshal said, "You're under arrest, you two boys, you were part of this too."

Wally knew it was going to happen, and was one step ahead of things.

Sam Abbott said, "But who will look after the horse, she just run a great race and she needs looking after. Please, Marshal?"

And Wally limped over on his stick and said, "I'll take her home for you, son. We'll take her back to your Livery in town, or deliver her out to your mother. I'll make certain nothing happens to her, is my assurance to you as a horseman — you got my word on it. And I hope now you'll tell the whole truth — and not *just* about the ringing in of horses. There's a little girl over there whose parents were murdered, and your brother Red told Deputy Slaughter who done it. You can tell the truth now without being killed — and I reckon you'll get a lighter sentence if you do so."

"Yessir, Mister Davis," said the wide-eyed young Abbott — for though he was being arrested, he'd realized something just then while Wally was speaking.

He'd been given his life back. And too, his mother was safe now.

Wally said, "Mary, little help here please, and you too, Lyle. Someone needs to lead Jessy Gillespie over there for a drink now, while they give me and Georgina the trophies."

"I'll lead her," cried Mary with pleasure. Then she looked at the big horse properly for the first time — her attention, of course, had been on Wally's mare Lulu til then — and to our eternal surprise, Mary cleared up the biggest mystery of all.

"Oh my," said the child, clapping her left hand over her mouth for a moment as she stared at the horse. "My goodness. The Dark Horse is smaller, but those ears are the same — and now there's the white on her legs — and goodness, the white on the legs is the same thing that happened, *that's* how our horse got her name — and goodness no, it *can't* be her — *surely* it can't — but then, *everything* seems smaller now, and perhaps it's just that *I'm* bigger than I was then — oh, goodness, it *can't* be — but *is it?*"

"Is *what* it, child?" I asked her. "Explain it, we're all on the edge of our seats. Just *tell* us, whatever it is."

"Why, this horse looks *exactly* like the one my dear Daddy brought home, just a few weeks before he was killed. When I asked where she was, Mister Benson insisted the horse had run off in fear — I always assumed the mean man had sold her, you see? But look! The Dark Horse looks exactly like *our* horse — oh goodness, it *is* her, it *is*. This isn't *The Dark Horse* at all — this is *Lady Magic-Foot Tall-Ears,* that's who it *is!"*

We all watched on, awestruck and dumbstruck and everything-else-struck — *speechless by what we was hearing, would be my main meaning* — not just me and Wally, but the Abbotts too, and Georgina, and even the Marshal.

Mary hugged the horse now, with the tears streaming out from her eyes, overwhelmed as she was. "She belongs to my daddy," she said. "And now she's come *home.* You're home now, my dear Lady Magic-Foot Tall-Ears. You're home, you're finally home."

CHAPTER 53
THE TRUTH, THE WHOLE TRUTH...

F unny thing — in all the commotion out at the racecourse, Sheriff Cal Pettygore somehow slipped quietly away, and it seemed like he'd disappeared. But young Emmett Slaughter's no fool, he hightailed it to the train station, and found the Sheriff boarding the train that was headed for San Francisco.

Pettygore then drew his weapon and threatened to make things interesting, but young Emmett had already outthought him — as Emmett reasoned with Cal, one a'the other Deputies came up behind the escapee Sheriff and pistol-whipped him.

Turns out his wife had been telling the truth — Cal's brain really WAS only half the size of the Mayor's.

They dragged Pettygore off of the train and locked him up in his own hoosegow, on a charge of murdering young Red Abbott in cold blood. I suggested they charge him with stupidity too, but Emmett said if they made it an offense he'd be forced to lock up the whole town, just for voting Mayor Fisk and Sheriff Pettygore in in the first place.

The Abbott boys told the whole truth soon as the Federal Marshals took 'em away. We didn't get to hear it til we watched the trial three days later — Judge Wilcott presiding. Seemed like half the dang town came to see the Mayor get his comeuppance — *we* sure weren't gonna miss it. In the end, after quite some discussion, we even took Mary.

We'd have preferred she not be subjected to it, but she had a right to decide for herself — and she really wanted to be there to see justice done.

The story of the previous ring-in made for some mighty interesting listening, even for Wally, who already knew more-or-less what must have gone on.

Turned out the Abbotts' Pa — Delvene's husband, Henry Abbott — had gone to San Francisco as a late added extra to the whole thing.

Mayor Fisk had already bought Jessy Gillespie, but another feller was secretly training her, in a small town outside San Francisco. Henry had done this shady sort of work before, dyeing horses for ring-ins as far away as Kentucky. He was considered the best there was at it, so when the trainer couldn't make the dye stick, they had Henry go all the way to San Francisco to do it — the occasion being as important as it was.

Jessy Gillespie had won in a romp as the poorly performed filly, Thunder Cloud — and they got her outta the place soon as ever they could. Henry had been instructed to shoot Thunder Cloud, so she could never be found and compared to the horse that had won the big race.

But with Jessy Gillespie being also highly valued to breed with, they wanted to keep her, a'course, despite it being a risk.

Thing was, it was Henry Abbott's job to minimize that risk, by taking Jessy Gillespie home to his ranch and keeping her hidden away.

But as both Abbott boys testified, their Pa loved horses too well to go killing one — Henry took a big risk for the sake of those horses, and secretly took them *both* home. But when he took 'em off the train in Cheyenne, and got 'em back to his Livery under cover of darkness, he was mighty worn out from the awful long train journey — not to mention he'd hardly slept a wink them three days from all a'his worrying.

He put the horses in the stables, told his son Red to take the one in Stable Three to their ranch, and sell the one in Stable Four to anyone who wouldn't be likely to take her nowhere near a racecourse.

Needless to say, he'd put the wrong horse in the right stable — or maybe the other way round, now I think on it some.

And a'course, Mary's Pa bought the horse that Red offered him next day. She was sweet-natured and quiet, as thoroughbreds go, but way too slow to race or even breed with, he was told. And Jacob Wilson snapped her right up, bargain-priced as she was.

What with Henry being busy in town, building up the Livery all fancy, and also having more trips to make to the

East to buy other horses, he never knew Red had sold the wrong horse til a couple of months later.

The Mayor wanted to go see the horse, but when he came out there, they saw right away the horse's ears were all wrong.

Threats were made, as you'd expect — the Mayor told Henry Abbott to fix it next day or he'd die. Henry visited the Wilson place, offered triple the money he'd paid for the horse, but Mary's Pa told him no.

When describing that day for the Judge, Ben Abbott said, "Mister Wilson made himself clear. Told Pa his daughter loved the horse dearly, and he couldn't part with it for any amount we would offer."

The next day Mayor Reginald Fisk made them all go back there with *him* — all the Abbotts went, except for Delvene, who knew nothing about *any* of it.

When young Clarrie Abbott gave evidence, he was told to explain it in detail. "We rode on into their yard, just thinkin' Mayor Fisk was gonna make a huge offer to buy the horse back."

Then Clarrie choked up a little, had trouble going on.

Clarrie's mother was in the front row of the court, and young Clarrie turned to her then, the tears running free from his eyes, and he said, "None of us had no idea, Ma. And Fisk just said, *'Wilson, the price for the horse is a thousand, we're taking her now.'* Then Mister Wilson replies, *'I'm sorry you wasted your time coming out, Mayor. But my daughter loves that horse. Like I told Henry yesterday, thanks but no thanks, and goodbye.'* Then Mayor Fisk shouts, *'Goodbye it is then.'* And he pulls out a six-shooter, puts three bullets into the man, then two into his wife when she come runnin' out screaming."

Well, a'course, the tears burst on outta my dear little Mary when she heard them words, and her sobs just about broke our hearts.

We knew that if she attended the hearing, she would hear those terrible words — and it was the reason we did not want her to be here.

"Shall I remove her?" said the Bailiff uncertainly. He had no idea what to do, as Mary buried her face into Georgina's chest and kept sobbing.

But the wise Judge Wilcott said, "No, it's perfectly fine, Bailiff. It's completely up to the child — if she wishes to stay, we shall give her a moment to recover, or longer if needed. Indeed, we shall wait as long as it takes. Would you like an adjournment, Mary Frakes?"

Mary turned her head toward the Judge, wiped her eyes and plucked up the courage to speak. And in a small voice she said, "Thank you, Judge Wilcott, but no. Please carry on. Let us not delay Justice."

And she smiled at the Judge — the smallest and bravest of smiles — and he said, "Good girl. Now, let us continue."

CHAPTER 54
JUSTICE

When Clarrie Abbott was describing how the Wilsons was killed, he couldn't barely speak for how upset he was already — but when Mary howled he cried right along with her too, and he had to be taken from the courtroom, for he couldn't stop.

The Judge said, "Clarence Abbott is now excused. Prosecutor, you may now call Benjamin Abbott to take over."

Young Ben took the stand and swore on the bible, looking solemnly at the Judge, and then at his mother, then he got to speaking.

"We was all standin' too far from Mayor Fisk when he shot 'em. Not a thing we could do — what a shock. Then it was all over, and both them nice Wilsons was dead on the ground. It was me who run over and checked. It's a true fact that they both died instant — didn't suffer no longer'n a second or two. I can promise you that, Miss Mary, I swear it."

I had my arm around Mary's shoulders as we sat and listened, but it was Georgina who Mary leaned her head against — and she held *both* our hands.

"Red cried his heart out," Ben Abbott explained. "Damn Mayor threatened to shoot him, he was howling so bad. After, Red kept blaming himself for their deaths. And then two nights later, the Mayor shot Pa dead as well. No warning at all, same way as he killed the Wilsons. Then he tells us to go tell the Sheriff our Pa just shot himself cleaning his gun — and if we say different, he'll have our Ma tortured and burned. *I'm so sorry, Ma — Mayor Fisk gave us no choice, we had to protect you.* Then later, he told us if we ever said anything, he'd have Sheriff Pettygore charge *us* with murdering the Wilsons — and our own Pa as well."

The prosecutor sagely nodded his head, and as kindly as he could, said, "And your brother Redmond? Why was *he* killed?"

"Red couldn't take it no longer," said Ben. "It was eatin' him up somethin' terrible, knowing the little Wilson girl had no parents on account of him making a mistake with the horses. He wanted to tell Ma, but we couldn't. Then when Mayor Fisk told us to get Jessy Gillespie ready to run as a ring-in again — well, Red told him he wouldn't do it on any account. Told Fisk he'd go to the Law if he tried to force us to do it."

"And then?"

"The Mayor said he wouldn't be game — but Red did it. He always *was* the brave one, even though he was youngest. He went to the Sheriff — *Cal Pettygore there* — and Red told him the truth of it all."

"And then?"

"Pettygore told him to keep it a secret, and he'd come see Red in private that night at the Livery. Said we'd all have to be real careful, what with the Mayor being such a powerful feller."

"And that night?"

"We was there at the Livery together, all three of us. And the Sheriff comes in, sneaky-like, slips through the door and he shuts it behind him. Then he writes down all of our statements, and we think it'll all be okay — then he stands like to leave. But he goes for his gun, shoots Red just like that with no warning! Red bolts out the back door, and onto a horse he'd been keeping saddled most nights."

"What happened next?"

"That's about all of it really. Went just like when the Mayor killed the Wilsons and Pa. Sheriff tells us we're *dead* if we so much as say we were there, when he shot Red. That's the truth, that's all of it now — and so help me God, I'm an Abbott, we was *raised* to be truthful. I'm just glad it's all over, and you can string me up now for my part in it all."

Judge Wilcott didn't string no Abbotts up.

The Abbott boys got fined five-thousand each for their part in the ring-in, and suspended from racecourses for the next five years.

Delvene had sat in the court the whole time, not said a word up to that moment — but when them boys only got fined, she said, "Hallelujah."

Just spoke that one word out loud, but she turned to me then and she mouthed the words, *'Thank you, Frakes.'*

I only nodded and shrugged my old shoulders — I hadn't done nothin' really. Not sure why she thanked *me,* but I guess she felt like thanking *somebody,* so I didn't mind, I just nodded.

Sheriff Calvin James Pettygore was found guilty of murdering Redmond Abbott, and got sentenced to twenty years of hard labor — twenty years, with some a'the men who *he* had locked up.

He was middling-tough, Cal Pettygore — but he wouldn't last twenty years, I knew that right away.

And that damn filthy skunk of a Mayor — when Judge Wilcott sentenced him to hang soon as they could build a gallows, he wet his damn trousers and screamed like a pig that's been speared by an arrow.

I looked at our dear little Mary, and she didn't say anything — she just stared at the skunk as they dragged him out screaming, then put her little hands together and said a short mumbled prayer.

Then she stood, let out a big breath, closed her eyes and held out her two hands.

And holding my hand on one side and Georgina's the other, our little girl nodded her head and smiled a wise one — and we walked out into the street all together, and into the rest of our lives.

And we all knew it didn't make up for what happened, not really — but in some way ... some small way, at least ... Justice was done.

CHAPTER 55
CALL ME GEORGE

We had all won a whole lotta money that day at the races — and we put it to real good use.

Roy Grimm's wife had been unsuccessful in borrowing money from her family. But me and Wally won so much on his Cup horse, we just went and bought the place over on Love Street — the place young Roy had his eye on for a Livery and Saddlery.

Next day after the court case, we told Roy we'd bought it, and that it was to be his on interest free terms — payable when he could pay.

"No hurry," Wally told him with a chuckle. "We got plenty left over to last us awhile."

Poor kid musta got somethin' sizable stuck in his eye that very same moment — for it took him a minute or two to wipe it out, afore he could even look at us. And them dang eyes a'his kept on leaking while he shook our hands near to bits as he thanked us.

He wanted to run and tell his wife right away, but we

told him our loan conditions forbade it — instead, we made him go over there with us to help prepare the place first.

Georgina and Mary — each using a biggity helping of feminine artistic flair — painted up two big signs, before directing us men to nail 'em up on the front a'the building, right where the whole world could see 'em.

Then the girls declared the place ready, and sent Roy off to fetch his good wife.

She had told him a few nights ago that she was with child — so it was a *double* celebration, more-or-less. And when that girl seen the sign, she near passed out from the shock.

Grimm & Sons Livery it said on one side a'the building — and on the other side the sign read Cindy's Saddles & Tack ∼ Best Quality Leathergoods.

Well, with everything being so busy, that was the first time any of us had met her — but I tell ya, she was so happy she went from one to the other of us, hugging and kissing us all like we was her family, which it *sorta* felt like we was — and it seemed to me like *all* of us got somethin' in our eyes then, for we all had to wipe 'em dry more than once.

As for young Emmett Slaughter, he soon found himself busier than ever. After jailing the County Sheriff, Judge Wilcott tasked young Emmett with heading up the Cheyenne Sheriffs Office until the elections next month.

There was grumblings about that from two a'the other Deputies — the two shadiest fellers, those closest to Sheriff Cal Pettygore. Roebuck and Rudd was their names, and they had reputations for playing loose with the truth. The very next day after Pettygore got sentenced to jail, they came to Emmett and threatened him not to run in the election — leastways not if he planned on staying alive.

Emmett woulda fired the pair if he could, but he ain't got jurisdiction to do so. Judge Wilcott said he can't do nothin' about it, not unless they make their threats in front of a witness. So for the moment, young Emmett's just bein' careful, and I'm helping him out some with that.

Other interesting thing, Emmett's father turned up in Cheyenne. The Slaughters invited us over for afternoon tea the next day, so we could all get to know him. All I *really* knew of the man was what Emmett had told me — "My Pa has followed your career for many years, Lyle, and aways spoke highly of you, ever since I was little. I'm sure he'll be thrilled to finally meet you."

I just hope he don't make a big thing of meeting me. Ain't like I'm nothin' special.

They were inside the house when we arrived, and didn't come out onto the porch until we'd already tied up our horses and walked up the stairs.

"Lyle Frakes..." Emmett said when he introduced us, "...this is my father, George Slaughter."

Well, I looked at the man, and you coulda knocked me down with a barn swallow's tailfeather — I knew him!

Oh, I knew him alright, but not by the name George Slaughter. And no doubt, he knew me too, though he didn't let on.

"Mister Slaughter," I said. "Your son's told me *everything* about you, I reckon. I'm happy to finally make your acquaintance. Please call me Lyle."

And the feller said, "Told you *everything,* has he?

Sounds like a *lot*. Well, I guess he knows all there *is* to tell. Pleased to make your acquaintance, Lyle. And I *do* hope you'll call me George."

"George," I said, shaking his hand as I looked into his mirthful eyes.

"I was hoping you might be able to help me some, Lyle. Or perhaps find someone who can. Old friend a'mine's found himself in a deadly situation, you see — and the Law says there's nothin' they can do."

"Well, we best talk about that," I said. "See if there's some way we can help."

And I sat down to coffee and a slice of Jeanie Slaughter's best pie — with the first man I ever arrested for murder, just about thirty-five years back.

Things was about to get interesting.

The End

THE DERRINGER

If seven-year-old Roy Stone had done what his Ma told him to, he'd never have known the truth of what happened at all.

He'd never have seen the double-cross, never have witnessed the murders, never seen the killer's blowed-apart finger. But the poor kid saw the whole rotten thing, and watched his mother die on the floor.

"I'm going to kill you," little Roy cried at the killer – but Big Jim only laughed with contempt.

But that little boy meant what he said – and what's more, he believed it.

He would grow up and kill that big man. That was all that now mattered.

Available as an eBook and in paperback.

WOLF TOWN

Cleve Lawson is a man for minding his business. But when he witnesses a stranger murdered by road agents, then the outlaws kill his best friend, Cleve decides it's high time he stuck his nose in where it don't belong.

As if all that ain't problems enough, he meets a tough yet beautiful woman who takes a shine to him – and a feller with fists of iron who takes unkindly to that.

Throw in a murderous road agent gone loco, an unfaithful dog, a wise-cracking Sheriff, and a range war between sheep and cattle men, and Cleve's got more troubles than an unarmed man in the middle of a gunfight.

Available as an eBook and in paperback.

FYRE

What if you went off to fight for what's right, and someone told your sweetheart you'd died? What if that same person told you that she was dead too?

What if that man up and married her? After secretly killing her family? And what if that man was the brother you trusted?

And what if, one day, you came home?

A story of trickery and cunning, of brotherhood and truth, and of war. Of bandits and shootouts and justice, and of doing what's right. Of a tall man who slithered, and a dwarf who stood tall as the clouds, and became Billy's friend.

It's the story of how Billy Ray becomes Billy Fyre – and how, seven long years after being told he'd lost everything, finally, Billy comes home, to fight for what's his.

Available as an eBook and in paperback.

WILDCAT CREEK

Toy Gooden always did think the best of the people he knew – that's how his troubles all started, and just kept on getting bigger.

When ten-year-old Toy takes the blame for a killing done by his best friend, it sets off a chain of events that's a never-ending passel of trouble.

Ten years on, wanted for a robbery and murder he didn't commit, and hated by his whole home town, Toy has to save Wildcat Creek (those very folks) from the bloodthirsty Gilman Gang. With no other help than a meddlesome twelve-year-old orphan, an ancient decrepit doctor, and a pesky tomboy outlaw who keeps insisting she wants to marry him, looks like Toy's got more troubles than a fingerless man in a gunfight.

Available as an eBook and in paperback.

Printed in Great Britain
by Amazon